A PRIDE OF KINGS

Juliet Dymoke

THREE CASTLES MEDIA

First published in Great Britain in 1978 by Nel Books
This edition published in 2017 by Three Castles Media Ltd.

Three Castles Media Ltd

Jacket design by Fourteen Twentythree

10 9 8 7 6 5 4 3 2 1

ISBN 978 1 52120 1749 Paperback 2017

For my cousin, Joyce Robertson

CHAPTER ONE

When he was six years old William stood in the midst of a group of hard-faced barons determined to see him hang. He was alone and very frightened, a hostage in the hands of his father's enemies, and his head barely reached the mail-clad thighs of these men, their kite-shaped shields seeming to him a wall of steel between himself and freedom. Looking up at them with a swift fearful glance he saw the grim expressions, the fierce moustaches where visors had been raised, and no mercy, no pity from any one of them.

But he must not show he was afraid, that much he had learned, and clasping his small hands behind his back he said. 'If you are going to hang me for my father's fault, messires, you had best do it now – for he will not yield to you.'

Someone at the back of the crowd laughed at the bravado of these words, only the foremost barons remained unmoved and William lowered his gaze to the forest of legs planted about him. He had seen a man hang once, seen the blood-darkened face, the protruding tongue, the enlarged eyeballs, it was a man his father had caught, a spy who had tried to poison the castle water. William had not wanted to watch, but his father was a hard man and stood with his hand on the boy's shoulder until the hanging figure ceased its jerking. Afterwards William had heard his mother protest, but she, gentle creature, had no power to sway her husband. William thought of her now and how she would weep if he did not come home. His hands tightened themselves into one hard knot as he waited, thinking of the rope and how it would feel, remembering that swaying, jerking man, the horror of that engorged face.

And then suddenly there was a movement behind and a tall man shouldered them all aside and came to the centre to look down at the boy. He had a face of great beauty, only the eyes were tired, the mouth drooping, and William knew who he was – King Stephen of England, for there was a gold coronet about his helm.

He looked sharply round the assembled barons. 'What answer did John the Marshal make to our demands?'

Roger, Earl of Clare stepped forward. 'He said, sire, that he will not, despite his agreement, yield to your terms. He will hold the castle of Newbury in the name of the Empress and as for this hostage, he says he has the hammer and the anvil yet to make more sons.'

A rare expression of anger crossed the King's face. 'Unnatural father! Has he no love for his own flesh?' He went down on one knee. 'Come here, boy.'

William came to him. Despite the anger he was not afraid of this tall man, still so handsome even in his fifties. But tears had threatened him at the harsh words of his father and he put up one hand to scrub at his eyes.

'Child,' Stephen said, 'you know that your father has betrayed me, and you too? He gave his promise to yield that castle to me, and you as a hostage for his word, and now he will not keep it. What must I do?'

William looked over the King's shoulder towards the grey walls, the raised drawbridge, the battlements alive with armed men secure behind their bastions. His father had supported the Empress Matilda, grand-daughter of William the Conqueror, in her struggle to win the throne from Stephen. Now that her son Henry, Duke of Normandy, was in England and winning where she had lost, John the Marshal thought he would better serve his own interests by holding out and waiting for the vigorous young Duke to relieve him – and if his own son was sacrificed in the attempt it did not seem to worry him unduly. William thought of his mother, and then of his elder brother John. Would John mind if he died? John was always so busy now, learning to be a squire, that he no longer had time for play. William found himself longing to be back in the busy courtyard, chasing the hens and ducks that wandered freely while waiting for the pot, talking to the men-at-arms, fed sweetmeats by the cook, and he yearned for all the familiar things of home instead of having to stand here while they talked of hanging him.

Yet the King looked kind. William swallowed the tears and said, 'Will you hang me, sire?'

Surprisingly Stephen was smiling. 'I don't know, William. Do you think I should?'

'No, my lord, for when I am grown I may serve you well.'

The King laughed outright at that. 'Why, so you may, and you have too good a wit for these knights to strangle it with a rope. Do you play at knucklebones, William?'

Startled, the boy said that he did.

'Then we will play together.' Ignoring a half uttered protest from one of the mailed knights, he went on, 'Come, sit down on the grass with me and tell me what else you like to do.'

So on the slope below the unyielding castle they sat down together, the King removing his helm and sending his barons to attend to the recommencing of the siege. When one began, 'My lord, this boy's life is forfeit, John the Marshal –'

'Is a fool,' Stephen finished blandly, 'not to know what a fine courageous lad he has here.' He demanded that some knucklebones be found for them and the barons dispersed, but there were black looks and further mutterings.

William cared nothing for these things while this kindly prince continued to smile at him. He did not after all, want to die on a bright June day when he was no more than six years old.

This was all many years ago now, but on a gusty March morning in 1168 outside the walls of Boulogne it came briefly to his mind, for he was joined by Gilbert de Clare, Earl Roger's son, and Gilbert was very like his father. William's own father, for whom he had felt no love since that morning at Newbury, was dead these four years, his mother even before that, and his brother John was marshal of England in his place. The year after they had sat together on the grass Stephen died and Duke Henry had become King Henry II, William had been sent to his father's cousin, William of Tancarville, following the custom that boys should be brought up in other homes than their own. Tancarville was Chamberlain of Normandy; a dry man sparing of speech, he had nevertheless done his duty well by the boy, and as William developed an ability far beyond average in the handling of every sort of weapon there also developed a somewhat inarticulate friendship between them. He saw his father no more than once after he was released, but of his captivity at King Stephen's court he had happier memories. Whatever they might say now of that ineffectual King, whose weakness brought such misery upon England that men said Christ and his Saints slept, he at least remembered Stephen with affection and paid for a mass to be said for his soul every year on the anniversary of the King's death-day.

When he was old enough he travelled Europe earning his bread by his sword and gaining experience both as a mercenary and as a combatant in any tournament he could find, living on the prizes he won and sold. These wild skirmishes had as yet few rules: it was not intended that men should die in them though there were often casualties, for a live captive brought the ransom that a corpse could not. William learned how to take the best advantage of the combats, how to measure his opponents, how to gain the best prizes. Men began to look for him when a tourney was announced, eager to test their skill against his.

This last spring, however, he had returned to England at the request of his dead mother's brother, Patrick Earl of Salisbury, a bluff plain man with a stomach blown out from overmuch fondness for ale. Salisbury was commanded by the King to lead an expedition to quell some rebels who were terrorising the country around Lusignan at the instigation of their Count, and he and his nephew had landed at Boulogne to find a tournament about to take place. It seemed that King Henry and his Queen were visiting the Count of Boulogne and that he had organised this entertainment for them, the range of the fighting strictly limited.

William had paid his two marks to enter and stood now some distance from the walls. He could not afford a body servant but he had offered a lad a penny to carry his arms and look after them inside the enclosure. The boy, towheaded and unwashed, grinned up at him and handled his shield and helm with awe and William ruffled his hair – the incident at Newbury had caused him to be kind to children.

It had rained a little in the night, enough to soften the earth, but now the sky was clear, the bright March sunshine surprisingly warm. Despite the early hour the enclosure was filling rapidly with young men eager to try their skill, seasoned knights preparing for the form of entertainment that they preferred above all else. Common folk were crowding the walls of the town for a spectacular view of their betters, clothed in chain mail, carrying brightly painted shields and armed with swords and lances, battering each other into a state of exhaustion, and if at the end of the day there were a few casualties so much the better. Some spilt blood added to the excitement.

William nodded to Gilbert 'I see there is a stand erected for the King – this is to be a more ceremonial affair than most I suppose.'

Gilbert shrugged. He was a short wiry youth, with dark hair and a dark stubble on his chin. 'For all the King won't have jousting in England, or in Normandy, that's not to say we don't organise a few tourneys on the quiet. We may surprise him today.'

'I doubt it – I imagine there is little that goes on that he is not aware of. Is your father here?'

'Yes, I'm to attend him. I hope the day goes well for you, William.'

'I hope so too. My purse is nearly empty – as usual.'

Gilbert gave him a broad grin. Well, it never stays that way for long. Do you remember the day at Liege? When we were so in debt we could hardly pay for our dinner? Those knights who attacked us during the dinner hour will remember their treachery, eh?'

A smile flickered across William's face. He too relished that memory when, surprised without their armour, he and his companions had had to beat off an attack and he had rushed into the fray to pull a nobleman off his horse and carry the man, armour and all, into the farmhouse where they were eating. The knight brought a high ransom and they were able to pay their debts and eat well for a fortnight.

'I wonder who will oppose us today,' he said. 'I think I

saw Sir John de Valence and Sir Robert Buckley over there. I have need of another horse, Gilbert. Did you notice who owns that chestnut percheron – do you see, towards the right of our foes for today? I could not see what arms his master bore.'

Gilbert shaded his eyes from the sun and then burst out laughing. 'By God's feet you are confident. That horse belongs to my uncle, Richard Strongbow.'

William was unperturbed. 'Is he considered a great fighter? I have not heard.'

'When you see him, you will think not. But he is no mean hand with a sword. And have you not thought you might lose this beast of yours?'

'No,' William said honestly. 'I have not lost a horse yet – and what other way have I to make my living? A landless younger son must provide for himself. I am not the heir to vast lands and an earldom as you are.'

Gilbert shrugged. 'It will be many a day before I succeed to them – my father is a lusty man and keeps me short in the purse. I'd best go and find him or I will yet again get the rough edge of his tongue. I suppose you will win a horse today – my uncle's or someone else's?'

'Will you wager on it?'

'Not I,' Gilbert retorted. 'I know you too well, William.' He glanced with something like envy at the tall figure beside him. William Marshal was to his mind everything a man should be – well-made and strong with a face not handsome but with even pleasing features and a skin turned brown from the outdoor life he lived and with eyes that were blue, steady and unflinching, and a mouth that could smile suddenly when one least expected it. William's hair was brown and thick and a moustache covered his upper lip though his chin had been freshly shaved this morning. It seemed to Gilbert who was not

'Oh, he does,' Will assured him, 'on the field. I hear he is in straits again with the moneylenders. They say he spends too much on lavish living and on his back - and you know he lost most of his estates for supporting King Stephen.'

That name stirred William and he looked with fresh interest at the man he meant to make his main opponent today. His brother John, carrying his marshal's staff, came past, a worried frown on his face for the Count of Flanders was not yet here and would take offence if the tourney began without him. He gave William a brief nod. They had met only twice in the last ten years and were as strangers. 'I hear you bear yourself well at these affairs,' he said curtly, 'but remember your place – you are not yet knighted.'

He hurried on not waiting for an answer, and William gave his companion an amused look. 'Do you suppose that was meant to wish me well or a hope that I might fall off my horse?'

And then there was no more time for talk as to the sound of a horn the Count of Boulogne led his illustrious guests to a stand erected for them. When he reached his seat King Henry turned and paused for a moment. He was a strong heavily built man with a bullet-shaped head under his crown, and his keen eyes glanced alertly round the large space marked out for the tourney. By his side the Queen whom he had wrested from the French King turned also to look at the crowds, the field bright with fluttering pennons, the sun glinting on steel. Eleanor was still beautiful, her dark hair encased in a crespine, a circlet of gold set on it, her body, still slender after bearing him eight children, sheathed in blue velvet, white sleeves hanging down, a jewel fastening her purple mantle. She had brought her husband great wealth and all the vast domains of Aquitaine and she had given him four stalwart sons and three daughters, the first of these already gone at twelve years of age to her wedding in Germany. Eleanor reached out to take the hand of her youngest daughter, her namesake, as the child climbed the steps, while her other daughter Joanna followed with her brothers, the handsome frivolous Henry, the more sturdily made Richard who at eleven already seemed likely to have all the striking Plantagenet looks, with his crisp red-gold hair and vivid blue eyes, and Geoffrey, ten years old and with the promise of the same good looks. Only the baby John was not present for he was little more than a year old and still in the charge of his wet nurse. With this bevy of children was also Princess Margaret, daughter of the King of France and already joined in wedlock to Prince Henry, though they were too young to consummate the marriage as yet, and her sister Alice who was destined to be Richard's bride.

With much laughing and chatter the royal party seated themselves in the stand beneath a banner showing the lions of England and Normandy, a symbol of the greatness of Henry, King of England, Duke of Normandy and Aquitaine, Count of Maine and Anjou, and the greatest thorn in the side of Louis of France – Henry Plantagenet, the begetter of a new line, the men who would bear the *planta genesta,* the sprig of broom. He sat now sprawled in his chair, a man of immense energy, clever, ambitious, autocratic, born to dominate, demanding obedience and unquestioning loyalty, and when he got it, inclined to be generous. He made a joke about his eldest son's eagerness to fight, bidding him watch well and learn. On his other side sat the Archbishop of York, on a brief visit from England and high in the King's favour since that disastrous quarrel with the

Archbishop of Canterbury now in exile. Henry did not want to think about Becket, that one-time boon companion and friend who had so inexplicably turned against him, thrown all his gifts in his face, and who now lived among the monks at Sens, gaining sanctity in the eyes of the world, encouraging the picture of outraged virtue and gaining the friendship of Pope Alexander in a manner which made Henry grind his teeth with rage. But he had a scheme in his head – it was seldom that he had not – to make Thomas Becket stir himself, and for a moment his alert eyes rested on the figure of his heir.

Two groups of knights began the contest, riding hard at each other with lances couched, and it became a wild struggle with mounted men controlling their horses with their knees. If a man fell and could not remount he fought on foot, but if a knight could seize the reins and drag the horse clear it became a prize. An even greater prize was to take a captive but most of the contestants avoided this. The air was filled with the clash of metal against metal as they battered at each other, and in the pauses between bouts the ladies clapped and received chaplets from their favourite knights. It was a great deal more orderly than the tourneys William was used to in Germany, but he waited a little while before entering, reserving his strength until he saw Strongbow mount, bearing the red cross of the Clares on his shield.

William mounted himself, took his shield from the boy, settled his helm on his head and held out his other hand for his lance.

'Good fortune,' Will said, 'and God send you are not brought back lying on your shield.'

He rose into the mêlée using his lance to some effect and when it shivered drew his great sword, his favourite weapon.

He drove off a knight who swayed violently in the saddle but without falling, kicked out at a man on foot who tried to wrench at his reins and pull his horse down, the familiar excitement seizing him; he could feel the heat in his face, the strength in his arm, and with it the knowledge that he was as skilled as any man there.

The Earl of Salisbury, nursing a bruised shoulder, made his way to stand beside the Chamberlain of Tancarville. 'You've taught my nephew well,' he remarked. 'I'll wager you never had a keener pupil.'

'Aye, and I'll tell you this,' Tancarville answered in his clipped voice, 'I've not in all my years seen a fighter like him. Mark me it will matter nothing that he has no lands – he will win all by his sword. And I tell you another thing, my lord Patrick, he may be ambitious – indeed he is – but he is neither greedy nor grasping. I wish I had more squires like him.' He hitched his gown about him, wishing that the pain in his joints that was insidiously taking possession of them these days would cease, that his own time with the sword and the lance was not over. His lean, hard features lit with a rare light, 'By God's bones, that was well done. He has broken Strongbow's lance. Turn, William, again! You have him!'

'Holy Saints!' Earl Patrick exclaimed. 'We will all have to look to ourselves when he enters the lists.'

In the field William, though he had not heard his tutor's words, was pressing home his advantage. Pursuing the Earl of Pembroke on the edge of the mêlée, he raised his shield to ward off a wild blow, there was a roar from the crowd as he rocked momentarily in his saddle, and then it was he who caught Strongbow on the shoulder, sending the Earl slithering sideways and out of the saddle. For one moment his foot caught in the stirrup and then he was free and rolling away on the ground, out of reach of the plunging hooves. William leaned forward and seized the reins of the percheron, dragging it clear of the fighting. Then he was cantering away with it to the edge of the field where, to an even louder roar from the watchers, he gave his prize into the care of Will FitzHenry before returning to the fight.

At last towards noon the heralds called a halt. Many knights, blown or horseless, had sought refuge in the wicker pens on the edge of the ground and William found he was among the few still left in the thick of it. While the judges conferred he stood leaning on his sword, aware of a certain pleasant weariness, an ache in his right arm that he would not have exchanged for all the luxury in the world. He was only half listening to Will's excited praise of his efforts when the Earl of Pembroke came over to him.

Richard Strongbow had walked from the field, little more than bruised by his fall, but there was a rueful expression on his face. 'Well, Messire Marshal, you have done well today. I'm not often unhorsed.'

'I must admit, my lord, that I'd set my mind on your percheron.'

'And you won him fairly, though it has put me in difficulties – I've to ride for the coast tomorrow and my purse is too lean for a mount of that quality.'

William's slow smile came. 'My lord, I can't credit that.'

'You may not credit it, but I have creditors enough to prove it,' Strongbow answered humorously. 'Well, he's yours and I'll have to hire me a mule to bear me to Calais.'

William hesitated, but only for a moment, aware of a sudden liking for this man. Then he said, 'Keep your horse, my lord. I will claim the debt another day for I see we are in like straits now.'

The Earl's eyebrows went up. 'You are singularly generous, William Marshal, and I thank you for it. A loan it is and here is my hand on it – for I must get to England. Will you drink a pot with me later?'

The horns sounded again and when there was at least partial silence the marshal announced in a resounding voice that his brother was the winner of the particular laurels for the day.

'Holy Cross!' Strongbow said, 'I am not shamed to have lost to the day's champion.'

William went forward, not without a certain surge of pride, and as he passed his brother, the marshal said in a low voice, 'Conceit will not commend you, brother, so show a proper reverence. And keep guard on your purse when you have it. Do not look to me to furnish your enlarged ideas.'

William suppressed the desire to laugh, and not answering his brother went up the step to the King's chair.

Henry leaned forward, the sun glinting on his close-cropped red hair, his rather protruding grey eyes fixed on the winner. His hands, which held the purse, were rough and reddened, but they glinted with jewels, while his doublet and short Angevin mantle were of the richest velvet, though their fit left something to be desired for this energetic man drove his tailor to distraction by refusing to stand still for more than a few seconds at a time. He held out the prize to William and his smile showed large uneven teeth.

'Well done, Messire Marshal. We shall have to find some place about us for you. Will you serve me?'

'In any way your grace desires,' William answered and bent the knee. Was this at last what he had hoped for – the landless man whose only chance to rise in the world lay in catching the eye of the King? He received his purse and became aware of the warm, dark eyes of Queen Eleanor upon him.

'Who better to teach our sons the use of arms?' she suggested, and unfastening the brooch from her mantle, she held it out to him. 'Take this gift from me, Messire Marshal. You have given us good entertainment today.'

William cradled it in his hand. It was of amethysts fashioned in the shape of a sprig of broom and set in a circle of silver, and the thought came to him that however hard pressed he might be he would never part with this, a Queen's gift.

Henry rose from his seat. 'You are marching out with your uncle of Salisbury to deal with the rebels at Lusignan, are you not? Then come to me when you return. I'll not forget what we have said. The care of our sons is most vital to us.' He gave his eldest son a quick smile of surprising sweetness, and offering the Queen his arm led her away out of the stand.

William had stood aside, bowing low, but the moment they were gone he was besieged by the young princes all talking at once, and it was Henry who turned fiercely on the others crying out, 'I am the eldest – Messire Marshal shall teach me first and I shall beat you both.

'Messire –' he turned eager blue eyes on the victor, 'Messire, you will not forget? You will come back?'

There was something about the boy that was immensely appealing and William answered without hesitation. 'I will not forget, my lord – even if your father had not commanded it, I would come back.'

Late that evening, with Richard Strongbow and his nephew Gilbert, and young Will FitzHenry, William went into the town that clustered around the slopes of the castle and to an inn where they stayed drinking until long after curfew, relaxing in pleasant company, talking over the events of the day, Gilbert repeating a somewhat scurrilous tale about Archbishop Roger of York that sent them all into shouts of laughter. At length Will slid under the table, overcome by cheap Rhône wine, and Strongbow offered to haul him back to the castle as he himself must be away by first light.

'I forgot,' William said in a slightly muddled voice. 'You are going back to England – on some mission for the King, my lord?'

Strongbow gave a low laugh. 'I hardly know, but his grace has given me permission to aid King Dermot of Leinster to regain his kingdom. Perhaps if I succeed in Ireland, King Henry may restore my English lands to me. I would like to end my days as lord of Pembroke castle instead of wearing an empty title.' He paused, one arm about Will who was displaying a tendency to giggle and blinking owlishly in the light of the guttering candles. The tavern was empty now save for themselves, and the landlord, wiping his hands on a grimy apron, was clearly hoping they would all go home. Strongbow added, 'You were generous to me today, William Marshal. If I have good fortune, I will be generous to you – maybe I will need a castellan at Pembroke, or perhaps you would prefer to see some fighting in Ireland?' But it was a rhetorical question and the corners of his mouth turned upwards as he held out his other hand.

William took it in a strong grasp. There was an odd moment of silence. The question was one that he could not answer now, but somewhere at the back of his mind it seemed to him that he would remember the words of Richard Strongbow.

When they had gone Gilbert hiccupped and said with his slight stammer that became pronounced when he was in his cups, 'My uncle must n-needs mend his fortune, and he will, b-by God – he's a C-Clare! Well, I'm for a night's wenching. C-come, let's see what sport we can find.'

An hour or so later William lay on a straw pallet in a house where a certain creaking sign hung over the street, and listened to the even breathing of the girl at his side.

He was satiated with success, with the day's triumph, with promises for the future beyond what he had dreamed of, with wine and now with the body of this girl lying close to him. He had a rich purse, several prizes, including Strongbow's saddle which he would sell for his keep, a Queen's jewel which would never leave his possession, and in the flush of youth though he might be, he was aware that he cared little for the moments of passion. It was what he had achieved today that filled his mind.

The girl stirred and turned towards him, sliding her arm around his strong muscled body, murmuring that he was a fine fellow, but he pushed her away, cool now that passion was satisfied, and slipping from the bed he pulled on his clothes. Then, leaving a coin on the stool beside her he went out into the night, and ignoring the curfew walked up the street to the lodgings he shared with his uncle.

To be tutor in arms to the heir to the throne of England – ah, that would be something and it was that thought that occupied him in the darkness under the brilliant starlit sky. A cat, scavenging on a midden, yowled at him as he disturbed her. William kicked some unsavoury rubbish at her and walked on, a faint smile on his face. The day had been a turning point, he was sure of it, and he flexed his muscles in anticipation, with no desire for sleep.

CHAPTER TWO

But he was not yet destined to achieve his ambition. A month later he was struggling back to painful consciousness to find himself lying on an evil-smelling pallet in a cell into which only a little daylight filtered through a narrow slit in the circular walls. As memory came back he put out a hand to feel the wound in his thigh and brought it away wet with blood, his hose sticking round the oozing hole. If this bleeding was not staunched he might lie here until he died, and he twisted his head towards the solid wooden door. There was a small grill in it but he could see no one outside; he was desperately thirsty and he called out, but there was only silence.

He tried then to remember clearly what had happened since the fight. He and his uncle with their men had been on the way to Lusignan and halting at a poor village found insufficient meat for their supper. They had gone hunting and were just returning when a party of Count Guy's men ambushed them. His uncle Patrick had no time even to arm and an enemy spear had buried itself deep in his chest so that he was dead before he reached the ground. There was a wild skirmish and William, already dismounted, could do no more than stand over his uncle's body and defend himself. There was a hedge of tangled briars and elder behind him and he had backed against this as the Count's men rode at him. He struck out, driving his sword into one horse's neck, catching another in the belly so that they and their riders came down in a kicking, heaving confusion. Somewhere he sensed some of his men still fighting, but the others must have run for in an incredibly short time he seemed to be standing alone. The end came suddenly. An enemy horseman riding round behind him jumped the hedge and plunged his spear downwards with great accuracy. William felt it drive into the fleshy part of his thigh and, panting with exertion, dizzy with the pain, his knees gave way and a dozen hands seized him.

Now he lay on this dirty pallet, bleeding, aware of waves of nausea and that he would have given all he possessed for a drink of water. How long he lay there he did not know and he wondered why, if they wanted him to die, they had bothered to bring him back – he had a vague memory of sprawling across a saddle, of hooves on a drawbridge, and it seemed to him he must lie in the Count's own castle.

At last when the light began to fade the door opened and a guard admitted a scrawny kitchen girl with a jug of water and a platter of unappetising gobbets of meat. From under her coif straggling dark hair hung down and smears of dirt hid the pallor of her face, but her eyes, frightened at first, showed a swift gleam of pity as she looked down at him. The smell of the stew added to his nausea and he reached out for the jug, drinking eagerly, the water running down his chin.

'Messire,' she whispered, 'your leg is still bleeding – can you not bind it?'

He shook his head. 'I've nothing –' but before he could finish the sentence the guard, a thickset bully of a man, came in and taking the girl by the shoulder twisted her away from the prisoner so that she gave a little cry of pain. 'Slut!' he said, showing blackened teeth, 'be about your business,' and a moment later the bolts shot into place behind them both.

William drank the rest of the water and tried to eat some of the meat. It was tough and with no seasoning but the warmth of it in his empty stomach gave him a little strength. He twisted his head and found it rested on his rolled up mantle, and struggling on to one elbow as a thought came to him he fumbled in its folds. To his astonishment his fingers came to rest on something hard, and he realised that by some miracle the men who had brought him in had not found his brooch, the Queen's gift. Perhaps they had bundled the mantle to support him on his horse and the clasp had been hidden in its folds. In any case he had it and freeing it from the mantle, he tucked it inside his stained gambeson where it would be even safer.

Then, exhausted, he fell asleep, but awoke in the dark hours to find his leg burning, and shoots of pain kept him awake for the rest of the night.

For another day he was left there alone. He could hear sounds of daily life, voices and tramping feet, horses' hooves and the jangling of accoutrements, but no one came to him, not even the kitchen girl, until evening when once more the door opened and Count Guy himself entered.

'Well, Messire Marshal,' he said in his grating voice, 'I have set a ransom of a thousand marks on you – a fair enough sum for so doughty a fighter. When I can spare a man you may send a message to someone sufficiently interested in your welfare to pay for it.'

William lay looking up at him. 'I shall be worth nothing to you if my wound is not tended.'

The Count gave his thigh a swift knowledgeable glance. He was a hard man who cared for nothing but his own person and his own land: if he gave homage to his overlord it was with the intent of keeping his word only when it suited him. At present it did not and he had a name for cruelty above the average, and not only towards his enemies. 'You are too strong to die of a flesh wound,' he retorted, 'and if you are in some discomfort maybe your friends will be all the more eager to redeem you. If not –' he gave an expressive shrug.

William looked at him with disgust. 'A man is not worthy of his knighthood who would ill-use an enemy to hasten his ransom. And my friends will pay nothing for my corpse.' But who would pay such a sum for him? His uncle now lay dead and his brother John had a mean streak that would send him counting his silver and deciding he could not afford it even for a brother.

He turned away to stare through the stone slit at the sunset sky outside, his mouth shut hard, and with a shrug the Count left him. But an hour later the kitchen maid came again and this time the bullying guard was not on duty and another man, rough but not unkind, turned his back while the girl brought a strip of clean linen from under her kirtle. What she lacked in skill she made up by her desire to help, and though William winced at her treatment as she washed and bound the wound, when she had finished he thanked her and asked if she had come at the Count's command. She shook her head, blushing, and he leaned forward to kiss her thin cheek, thus causing the blush to deepen.

That evening he was able to eat all the food. Slowly the inflammation subsided and a week later when the Count came again he seemed surprised to see the prisoner sitting up with his back against the wall. He repeated his demands and this time William asked him to send news of his captivity to his cousin of Tancarville, for although the Chamberlain was not a rich man he might be able to do something. Unfortunately, though he was not to know it, the messenger fell in with a party of drunken apprentices at an inn and after a rollicking night ended up stripped of purse and clothes and with a knife in his back. The Count's letter was swept on to the fire with the rest of the debris the next morning.

Slowly the summer days passed. His wound healed and William watched the golden dawns hoping each would bring a man riding from the north with a saddle bag containing the price of his release. But no one came and summer gave way to autumn and the darker days of winter. It grew bitterly cold in the tower where he was housed and they allowed him a small brazier and faggots of wood to keep himself warm, for he had nothing but his gambeson and his torn hose on his body. His gaoler in his surly way evinced a grudging admiration for his prisoner's fortitude for some of the men below had talked of his prowess in arms, and occasionally the fellow brought him snippets of news.

It seemed that Prince Henry had been allowed by his father to do homage to his suzerain, King Louis of France, for Normandy and Anjou, and that Prince Richard had been invested as Duke of Aquitaine. That would please the Queen, William thought, for it was obvious to all that Richard was her favourite child and it was her own province where lay her castle at Poitou that she loved most of all. William's longing to be free, to be part of these events, increased in him; the clamour of youth to be out of prison, astride a horse in the open air, grew to such an extent that his mind began to play tricks on him. His gaoler told him evil tales of this place, of a forest maiden, Melusine, who married a Count of Anjou and was seen to turn into a serpent; of another Countess who refused to go to Mass and when forced into the chapel by her husband's knights vanished when the Host was raised, and all that was left of her was the smell of brimstone. Truly the devil must know this place, William thought, and hastily crossed himself, but his sleep was disturbed and the winter wind outside made an eerie noise like the souls of the lost crying out in the darkness. Winter mists cloaked the world outside his window. He begged for a book, his cousin of Tancarville having seen that his education went beyond the use of weapons, and he was brought a volume of French poems filled with the ardour of love, the delight of youth in springtime, which did little for the peace of mind of a vigorous man of twenty-two locked in a room that he could cross in three strides. He tried to remember the tales sung by minstrels at Tancarville, of Roland and Oliver, of King Arthur and his castle of Joyouse Garde, of Galahad and the Holy Grail, but they only served to make his confinement more irksome. The Count decided to allow him out for some exercise and once a day his gaoler took him on to the castle walls where he could look out towards the north, over the stripped trees, the frozen water, the cold winter landscape. At Christmas he heard the distant sound of merrymaking, and wondered where King Henry and the princes were spending the festive season; he remembered the King's words to him, that he might instruct the heir to the throne, and he cursed the greedy Count whose forays had sent the Earl of Salisbury to do battle with him.

Even more he cursed him for not sending a second message after the first, which surely had never reached his cousin at Tancarville.

Spring came, and the trees grew green again, and he became even more desperate, but at last, late one afternoon when he was sitting on his pallet watching a strip of sunlight patterning itself on the floor, there were steps outside, though it was not yet the supper hour.

The door opened and Count Geoffrey stood there. 'Well, Messire Marshal,' he said, 'you are free to go.'

'To go?' William repeated in a stunned voice. He got to his feet, aware of a sudden swift pounding of blood through his veins. 'Who has paid my ransom?'

'Queen Eleanor and you may thank God for her generosity. I was becoming weary with feeding and housing you – I was considering selling you as a slave to the Moors.'

'Aye, my lord,' William said with outward calm. 'I did not look for mercy from you.'

'Did you not?' the Count queried in rather an odd voice. 'Perhaps I am not thought a merciful man – yet I have not had you thrown into a deep hole where men do not see the light of day again.'

To be free, to walk down the stair, out of this cursed turret, into the sunshine was so great a relief, so rich a joy that for a moment William, hardly hearing the Count's words, did not know how to contain his emotion. It mattered nothing to him that they gave him an old spavined hack to ride, that they returned neither his horse nor his weapons – nothing mattered but freedom and he turned his back on the grim castle, seeing the hack's head not to the north as he had dreamed of doing, but south towards Poitou, where they told him Queen Eleanor held her court.

CHAPTER THREE

'I am to be crowned,' Prince Henry said. 'William, do you hear? I am to be crowned King of England.'

'So I have heard, my lord. Yet it seems to me that your father still sits on the throne . . .'

'Of course he does,' the prince retorted impatiently, 'but don't you see, it is to ensure that I am the undisputed heir? Richard and Geoffrey are greedy, both of them, and this will make them do homage to me.' He laughed delightedly. 'Oh, I shall be glad to see Richard bend the knee. He is so stiff and serious and it was not fair to make him Duke of Aquitaine before I was given my inheritance.'

'Perhaps,' William said. 'My lord, do not hold your sword thus, you are not scything corn. Change your grip – so.'

'Very well. William, you don't seem to understand! I am to go to Westminster next month – to my coronation.'

'I understand very well, but we came out here to practise sword-play, and it is well for a king to be proficient in all the knightly skills.' But there was a faint smile on William's face as he spoke. They were in a field behind Winchester Castle, where other lords were either at the butts or throwing the spear. On the far side he could see his friend Will FitzHenry crossing swords with his half-brother. Prince Richard was now taller and more robust than his elder brother, but for all that William's own particular pupil was no laggard and was learning fast.

Since his release his fortunes had changed very much for the better. Queen Eleanor had received him graciously and furnished him not only with a better horse but with money for arms and clothes, and he had bent over her hand with a gratitude he was never to forget and which he could best repay by serving her sons. Soon after his arrival she had left her warm southern city where her subjects loved her as their Duchess, caring nothing that she was Queen of England and hating her husband as a stranger and an intruder. Now she was here in Winchester, preparing to attend the strange coronation, but William could see all was not well.

The King had had a succession of mistresses, his latest being the daughter of Eudes of Porrhoet – Gilbert de Clare confided to William that his own sister, a girl of great beauty, had lately been the object of the King's attention, but had had the wit to refuse him without bringing the family under his displeasure. Though the Queen accepted this situation as one not unnatural, nevertheless she was a proud woman and when a certain ugly rumour began to be whispered on the backstairs of the court, that the King was taking more than a fatherly interest in the French Princess Alice, his son's betrothed, it was not hard to see that the love she had once felt for her much younger husband was dying a swift death.

When William Marshal was made tutor in arms to her eldest son she had said, 'Messire Marshal, I am glad to hear it. He may have need of your loyalty.'

William was thinking of these words now as he paused, sword in hand, looking into the flushed face of the youth who stood before him. When Henry was crowned, when he had set his hands over his tutor's, where then did loyalty lie? To which king?

'Don't look so troubled,' Henry said. 'My father has enough to do in Normandy. I shall have England for my portion and you will be one of my chief advisers. Won't that please you?'

'If you think your father will relinquish the government of this land to you, then you are mistaken,' William answered frankly. 'You are but fifteen, my lord.'

'And a man,' Henry flashed. He rubbed his hand over his chin as if to be sure there was a slight sandy stubble there. 'If I were not he would not set the crown on my head. Stay by me, William – you gave your word.'

'I did, and I will not go back on it. But I do not see how you can be crowned now – the Archbishop is in exile.'

'Oh, Becket!' Henry retorted with a touch of impatience. 'Everyone is so concerned about him. Do you know, they even say he has begun to work miracles at Sens? Years ago when he was teaching me my letters, and a tiresome business it was, I liked him very well. He was not so stiff-necked then. But if he won't obey my father, he can't come back to England and what are we to do? Archbishop Roger of York will crown me – he has agreed. I shall choose the knights to bear my arms into the abbey. Will you carry my helm, William?'

'You honour me, sir.' The answer was formal, but William was nevertheless aware of pleasure, despite the misgivings. No one but the Archbishop of Canterbury had the right to crown a king, but it seemed as if Thomas Becket's quarrel with King Henry would never be mended, and nothing could stop this latest scheme to flout him. William could see the possibility of results following from it as inevitably as the rings of water from a stone thrown into a pool, and in the short time since he had become part of this boy's daily life he had grown to care deeply for him. Young Henry was eager to learn, a generous master to his household, easy-going and approachable, unstable perhaps beneath the charming surface, but he was, as William had just said, only fifteen. With this in mind he added, 'You would do well to remember that even when I do so, when the crown is set on your head, we are both your father's men still.'

'Of course.' In a gesture at once friendly and imperious the Prince laid a hand on his companion's arm. 'Dear William, you see trouble where there is none. God aid us, what's amiss with Richard and Geoffrey?'

William glanced across to where the two younger princes had been practising at the butts. Apparently some argument had blown up, for, discarding their bows, they were now rolling on the ground together, punching and scratching at each other. With an exclamation William strode across at the same time as Will FitzHenry appeared from the opposite direction. 'Separate the cubs,' he said curtly. 'Enough, my lords, enough! Let be, I say.' He leaned over and heaved Richard up and away from his brother while Will grasped Geoffrey who, with arms still flailing, was no match for his older half-brother.

Panting and dishevelled Richard glared at William. 'What did you interfere for? I wasn't hurting him.'

'You were,' Geoffrey screeched. 'You nearly broke my arm, curse you – and you promised me that bow.'

'When you can shoot straight, which you can't yet.'

'I can – I can. Since you've become a duke you think you can do what you like, but you can't! I'll ask my father –'

'Oh, run to him if you will. Mother can hold her own with him and she –'

Geoffrey's face was scarlet. 'I hate you, Richard. You and mother are always scheming together –'

'Be silent, both of you,' Henry broke in. 'You are like a pair of snarling wolf cubs.'

Richard shook himself free of William's hold, relaxed now that the scrap was ended. 'This is none of your affair. If you think a crown on your head is going to entitle you to order Geoffrey and me –'

'My lords!' William broke in sharply. 'It is not seemly that his grace's heirs should brawl like common tavern lads.'

'Is it not?' Richard broke into harsh laughter. 'Don't you know we Angevins are born to fight each other, brother against brother, father against –' he broke off, the laughter dying, and picking up his bow he turned his back on them all and strode off towards the postern gate, the sunlight turning his thick curling hair to a mass of gold.

With a shrug, Geoffrey added, 'He's right, you know, but we can be friends when we choose. Only today I do not choose.' Echoing Richard's laugher, but more lightheartedly, Henry thrust an arm through Geoffrey's, suggesting they visit the fletcher where he would buy him a finer bow and better arrows than Richard's.

The Earl of Leicester, who had been at the butts and seen the quarrel, came up in time to hear the last exchange. 'What a brood! I fear our lord the King has reared trouble for himself.'

'They are boys,' William said. Time and wise counsel will make better men of them.'

Robert de Beaumont raised one eyebrow. 'Do you think so? We had best pray you are right, but I doubt it.'

The coronation was a sumptuous affair. Archbishop Roger, well satisfied with himself since he had received the Pope's reluctant approval, set the crown on young Henry's red-gold head on the fourteenth day of June. It was whispered that the Pope had, at the insistence of Becket, sent a second letter cancelling his consent but whether this had ever been received no one knew for certain.

The ceremony and the days of celebration that followed were magnificent: no expense was spared. The common folk who had lined the streets to see the handsome youth ride by were treated to great casks of wine and whole roasted oxen as a gift from their new King, and William, walking with three other knights behind him into the abbey, forgot for a moment his misgivings.

In the months that followed the young King stayed in England, learning the business of kingship and attended by Archbishop Roger, the Earls of Leicester and Norfolk, and William was constantly at his side. Tidings came that the King and his exiled Archbishop had met at Fréteval, that there had been a reconciliation, albeit a chilly one, and that King Henry had given Becket permission to return home and in due course to crown the Young King a second time.

Henry's satisfaction at this was soon changed, however, and William came into his room on a bitter day in December to find him striding up and down in a furious manner reminiscent of his father. 'William!' He seized his arm. 'Have you heard –'

'What, sire?' William asked. 'I have only just come from my chamber.'

'The hall is always buzzing with gossips before ever I hear it,' Henry retorted. 'Do you know what Becket has had the impertinence to do? He has excommunicated Archbishop Roger here – for crowning me! How dared he? And he has ridden to Canterbury with bells ringing and people cheering, as if *he* ruled this land. Now he has sent a message that he is on his way to visit me, that he will come through London first, and my messenger says the common folk – stupid, gullible fellows – are coming out in their thousands to kiss his shabby robe and his muddy feet. I'll not have it – I'll not have it.'

At the end of this impassioned speech, he paused for breath, his face flushed and angry. In contrast Archbishop Roger, who had sunk down on the stone window seat, raised a face grey with fear. He was shaken out of his usual complacency. The letter of excommunication was lying in his cupboard and with it a threat to lay all England under an interdict so that every church door would be shut and nailed, the faithful deprived of the sacraments, the dying departing this life unshriven. He did not know what to do, torn by loyalty to a stem master, this boy's father, on the one hand and on the other, to his spiritual superior the Primate of all England supported now, it seemed, by Pope Alexander.

'I think,' he said at last, twisting the episcopal ring on his finger, 'I think we must await the commands of your royal father.'

A further blaze of anger shook the young Henry. 'I am king here now and Becket, and all of you, shall know it.' He flung himself down on the side of his bed, rich with red velvet hangings, the badge of his house embroidered there in silver, but the next moment he was up again, an imperious figure in long gown, embroidered sleeves trailing, a gold circlet on his head. 'Call me a clerk. I will send a message to the Archbishop that he is to bide quietly at Canterbury and cause no more stir. I will not have him riding about my kingdom, causing trouble among ignorant folk.'

The Archbishop bowed and withdrew, a tired and frightened man, and Henry turned, tucking his arm in a familiar gesture through William's. 'Come, let us go out. I hate such annoyances and an hour at the chase will blow all this away. I am right, am I not William?'

'I hope so, sir.' But the affair was disquieting and William followed his young master down the stair, wondering why Thomas Becket had taken part in a reconciliation only to do the very thing he knew would anger his royal master. The threat of interdict lying over them all was not pleasant. Like Henry, William was devout; he believed in the Church's care for souls. The holy chrism had been poured on Becket's head, making him their spiritual lord, their father in God – and the dividing line between that authority on the one side and material kingship on the other had become fine indeed.

They rode out into the cold crisp air, accompanied by several other lords, a gathering of young men all eager to follow another young man. The trees were white with hoar frost, ice on the puddles, twigs snapping beneath the horses' hooves. Henry had the ability to turn from one to the other with his quick smile, his anger forgotten in his love for the chase, and there was not a knight there who had not at one time or another received his generosity. He was lavish to his friends – William wore a short hunting mantle of green velvet trimmed with fur that the Young King had given him – and in a sudden rush of affection William felt only irritation that churchmen should make such a bother over what they called their rights.

The castle hall at Winchester was decorated with evergreen branches ready for the Christmas feast and the short December days passed quickly. Henry kept his court alive with his own merriment, playing the Lord of Misrule himself; he was a fair mimic and several high-born lords found themselves the butt of the company's laughter. And then, while the festivities were still in full swing, on the last day of the year when the first flakes of snow were drifting down, a muddied messenger burst into the hall at the dinner hour, crying out that he must see the King.

Henry had been about to take his seat on the dais and he paused, one hand on which gleamed a large ruby resting on the back of his chair. 'What is it?' he demanded. 'Why do you come into our presence in such a state?'

'Sire!' The man threw himself on his knees. 'The Archbishop is dead – murdered in his own cathedral at Canterbury!'

'Dead? Murdered?' Henry could scarcely get the words out. 'In God's name who could do such a thing?'

'Four knights, my lord – your father's knights – Fitzurse was one – they smashed his skull open, and men are saying that your father sent them –'

Years afterwards, looking back on that scene, William thought it was a turning point for them all. A few angry words, spoken by King Henry in a moment of exasperation against what seemed to be the treachery of a friend, had brought about that ghastly tragedy.

Christendom was shocked, revolted by the deed. The blood and brains of the murdered Becket, spilt on the steps of the choir in so bestial a manner, became holy relics. People swarmed into the church, pulsating with horror, to dip their kerchiefs into the blood, to touch the place of martyrdom in a fervour that swept the nation.

Young Henry left the hall, the meal untouched, and in his chamber above wept for his one-time tutor, forgetting his recent annoyance and cursing his father for being the author of so terrible and sacrilegious a murder. King Henry swore he had never intended the knights to take him so literally and did public penance, even allowing himself to be flogged by the smug monks of Canterbury, but it did little good. Thomas Becket became a martyr and nothing was ever the same again.

Some eighteen months later in the spring of '72 King Henry came to England and at Pembroke Castle the Earl of Clare entertained him. Young Henry was with his father and William, in his train as usual, renewed his acquaintance with Strongbow. He had ridden ahead to be sure all was in readiness and Strongbow greeted him as an old friend.

William took his outstretched hand. 'We have been hearing great things of you, my lord. It seems you have all Ireland at your feet.'

Richard de Clare gave him a wry smile. 'It is so indeed. I little thought when I wed King Dermot's daughter that in two years he would be dead and Leinster under my hand, though we had a hard fight of it at Dublin. I think I have won too much.'

'You may well say so,' William commented dryly. 'There is but one master after all, and he is not too pleased.'

'He sent us to subdue a pack of wild Irish rebels thinking to keep us occupied with lesser affairs, and we won a kingdom. We know him too well to believe he would like that!'

'Aye, he will not even allow his own sons to rule what he has given them. My young lord is very restless.'

'Is he so? Well, the cubs must be kept in order, I suppose, and I shall have to submit all I have won to his grace's pleasure. At least he restored my lands here, and it occurs to me, William, that I am in a position to repay a certain debt.'

'A debt? To me?'

Strongbow smiled. 'I seem to remember that I owe you a horse.'

'I had forgotten that. We are both in better case than we were then.'

Strongbow nodded, his eyes wandering round his domain. 'Thank God for it. This is a fine castle, is it not?'

They were standing in the doorway of the great keep, newly finished, the limestone fresh and gleaming in the evening sunshine. It was built on the highest ground within the inner ward so that from the roof there was a fine vantage point looking out towards the river and the busy quay and the way to the sea, or inland to keep watch on the marches. The outer court was large with massive walls to protect it housing a mass of wooden buildings, kitchens, storerooms, guest rooms, and tonight every available space would be crammed with the army King Henry was taking to Ireland. A magnificent place, William thought and wondered what it would be like to be lord of so great a holding with many manors and farms and tenants so that one might ride all day on one's own land.

He turned back to his companion. 'I've seen none better for defence. Are you expecting trouble from the Welsh princes?'

Strongbow gave him a grin that was distinctly boyish. 'I took some of their leaders and many of their men with me to Ireland and let them garrison my castles there – that is my way of protecting the marches. I learned something about strategy in Ireland.'

'And acquired a wife,' William added, smiling. 'Very politic, my lord.'

'It was, but more than that now. My marriage has been happy, William. Did I tell you that I have a daughter? Isabel is six months old now and will have a fine dower with Leinster in her gift and my Norman lands beside – unless I should have a son in due time. Maybe I'll give her to you for your bride!'

It was said in a humorous manner and William answered in the same tone. 'By the time she is grown, I shall be a greybeard, my lord – to her at any rate.'

'When did that ever make any difference to a marriage?' Strongbow retorted. 'And she will wed where I wish. But no doubt by then you will have captured an heiress anyway. I think you are on your way to higher favours yet, although,' he paused, 'you do not seem to want to win your way by the marriage bed.'

William shook his head, but he said nothing and Strongbow went on, 'And there is not a man in Europe to compete with you in arms, yet you have not asked for knighthood. What do you care for, William? I've often wondered.'

William leaned against the heavy jamb of the door, his eyes on the sunset sky. He was silent for some time and Richard de Clare, who knew when to be patient, waited. At last William said, 'Chivalry, perhaps. I care for knighthood, Richard; that is why I have waited. When I take the vows I shall mean them. They are sworn to God, yet knights can act as Fitzurse did and de Moreville and the others. Do you know Hugh de Moreville once had a Saxon squire boiled to death for a trumped-up crime? Such men should have their spurs struck off.' He paused. It seemed to him that now, after two years, the unobtrusive reinstatement of the four men guilty of Becket's murder could be seen in two ways: perhaps the King felt a true sense of personal guilt and was not prepared to make the four scapegoats, or perhaps on the other hand, though he abhorred the actual deed he was glad that Becket was gone, that the quiet, amenable Abbot Richard of Dover should be Archbishop of Canterbury. William did not know, but the whole miserable affair had made him consider what chivalry should mean.

'Perhaps you are right,' Strongbow agreed. 'Fitzurse has been fighting with my men in Ireland. He's strong enough in battle yet his face has the look of a man who does not sleep easy at night.'

'That does not surprise me,' William said in his dry way. He smiled suddenly. 'I care for friendship, Richard – my young master's, yours, Gilbert's, Will FitzHenry's.'

'I know, but it is good to have a wife, children –'

'That will be as and when God pleases. For the present I have enough to do keeping my lord out of trouble.'

'Trouble?' Strongbow laughed. 'King Henry's brood were born to trouble and you will be in the thick of it.'

He was proved right only too soon. King Henry stayed in Ireland only long enough to ensure that Dublin and the Pale were well defended and that Richard Strongbow and other lords received their holdings as fiefs from the Crown, before returning across the channel, taking his eldest son with him.

Henry went reluctantly. He wanted to stay in England, to exercise his kingship, but with a brief 'no' from his father the country was left in the capable hands of the

Archbishops of Canterbury and York, the chief Justiciar Ranulf de Glanville, and a council of noblemen. He sulked on the ship and when they rejoined Queen Eleanor he was seen to be spending much time in whispered converse with her and his brothers, converse that ceased suddenly when anyone else came into the room.

Will FitzHenry, playing chess with William on the first night of their return, pointed out a young knight who owned the modest castle of Hautfort in Aquitaine. 'He is newly come to court,' Will said in a low voice, 'and one can't help liking him. He is a great singer of songs and can write a new one every supper time, but they are always – I don't know – more than they seem. Sometimes I think he means to fill men's heads with what would better not be there.'

William glanced across the hall in the direction Will was indicating and saw a handsome young man, dressed in scarlet sendal, many rings on his fingers. He had gathered a group of other young men about him where he sat on the steps of the dais below Queen Eleanor and some of her ladies. For a moment William paused to listen. The song was catchy, the tune such that every page would be whistling it on the morrow, and the words a clever mixture of fairy tale and fact William, though he had little interest in music except for dancing which he had grown to enjoy – one moved about in the dance and he preferred that to merely listening to tedious readings or poems – nevertheless found himself startled by the words. Bertran de Born sang of the fair Land of Aquitaine and its fairer Duchess, of the love of her people for her as their own, that they had no need of strangers from other lands.

'Is he a fool?' William asked abruptly but Will shook his head.

'No indeed. A subtle fellow, clever, and with such a

pretty wit one can't help wanting him to sing.'

During the next few weeks William made a point of talking with the knight and listening to his songs. Certainly Bertran was becoming renowned as a troubadour. Sometimes Prince Richard, who was also a good hand at composing, joined him and they entertained the court for many an evening.

Yet always there was an underlying note in Bertran's songs, the odd barbed dart that found its home, the innuendo that men might read if they wished into seemingly innocent words. More than once, as he listened, King Henry's brows drew together in a frown and there was little that he missed.

'Why do you do it?' William asked the minstrel one evening as he slid into a place at the table beside him. 'You stir up feelings that are best left alone.'

The dark attractive face of de Born wore a smile of satisfaction. 'Why, Messire?' he countered. 'Because where there is no conflict there are no great songs. Oh, I can write a verse for Queen Eleanor's Court of Love, but so can a dozen others. I have a wit for sharper things, and what better than to see the cubs sharpening their claws to challenge the old lion? It benefits me for the princes of this world to be warring with each other.'

William looked at him with distaste. He did not share Will's liking for this popinjay. 'You make mischief, Sir Bertram.'

'It is my trade,' the knight answered, and taking a portion of roast fowl tore at it with sharp white teeth. 'But the mischief was there before ever I put it into song.'

He was right, William thought. No one could fail to notice the uneasy atmosphere in the hall of late. This evening the usual rich dishes were served, the wine poured liberally, men and women at the lower tables talking loudly, and there were the usual bursts of laughter at some lewd joke or piece of titillating gossip. But it was observed that the King ate little, that occasionally he would rise and prowl about the hall listening to the talk, which died respectfully as he came past. The Queen sat with her eyelids lowered, Richard serious and silent by her side, Henry and Geoffrey with their heads together. Only the six-year-old John was at ease, laughing delightedly at the antics of the court jester and snatching his stick of bells to shake it furiously. 'I think,' William said at last, 'your wit is ill-timed. Sir Bertram.'

The knight gave him a sly look. 'Do you indeed, William Marshal? Pray that I do not some day turn it upon you.'

CHAPTER FOUR

Queen Margaret sat with her sister Alice, both of them busy with their embroidery for their mother had held the opinion that even princesses should not be idle, but Margaret's mind was not on the intricate little scene she was weaving, a hunting party with ladies and gentlemen in elaborate dress and with hawks above and hounds at their feet 'You are making that tree the wrong colour,' her sister said. 'I've not yet seen blue leaves.'

'Oh.' Margaret began to pull out the stitches. 'I was wondering where my lord is.'

Alice gave a little shrug. 'There is Messire Marshal passing the door. He will tell you – if you cannot beguile an hour with me without sighing for your bridegroom.'

Now that Margaret and Henry were of age they were living together as husband and wife, their happiness in their new state obvious to all, and her eyes were warm as she beckoned William into the room.

He came, bowing to the two princesses. Alice, he knew, was the cleverer of the two with a strong personality and a pair of hazel eyes that looked directly at a man with no hint of maidenly modesty, and he much preferred the quieter, gentler Margaret. 'How may I serve you, lady?' he asked, addressing his question to her.

'Messire Marshal, have you seen my lord? He promised to play at chess with me – he is teaching me the game – but he has not come and I wondered –'

'He is not in the hall, lady,' William told her. 'Perhaps he waits on his father.'

Alice said, 'Sister, you presume too much on a man's desire for women's company, even on Henry's for yours. Other occupations can soon wean them from us.' She leaned back on the cushions where she sat, taking a sugar plum from a dish beside her and nibbling it, savouring its sweetness. 'Is that not so, Messire William?'

He gave her a faint smile. 'If I say yes I shall be ungallant, but if I am truthful –'

'Oh do not be truthful,' Alice retorted lazily. The last thing we women want is plain truth. Margaret will find that it is so.'

The Young Queen shook her head. 'You are too devious for me. And Messire Marshal is in my lord's confidence.'

'I will look for him,' William told her. 'You have but to command me, your grace.'

He looked down at her, at the soft brown eyes, hiding now a trace of anxiety, and he wished that Princess Alice had held her tongue. What need to disturb this lovely girl's present happiness? He lifted her hand to his lips and held it there a moment longer than was necessary, before he went out and along the passage that led to the royal apartments. He was twenty-six now, of an age when many young men had taken wives and held lands of their own, begetting heirs to succeed them, but his path seemed to be set in royal service and, as he had said to Strongbow, he had not thought of marriage nor did he wish to. Of all the maidens he had danced with or talked to at the dinner table, only Queen Margaret seemed to him to be the perfection of all that womanhood should be, and those last words he had spoken to her were far more than a formal answer.

When he reached the entrance to the royal apartments he heard raised voices, the tone leaving no doubt as to the nature of the conversation, and he made at once as if to withdraw. His young master, however, was standing with one hand on the drawn-back arras and seeing him, commanded him to come in.

'William will bear me out,' he said imperiously. 'Since we came back I have had no money, not one silver penny from my realm and I am King of England. William, is it not true?'

Embarrassed, William stood in the doorway, hesitating to speak even in the face of such a demand, for the King, his highly coloured cheeks bright with anger, the grey eyes stormy, was prowling up and down the arched chamber. The Queen sat in her chair, her lips tightly pressed together, her eyes fixed on her favourite child, Richard, where he sat on a stool, his hands clasped between his knees, his mouth drawn down. Geoffrey leaned against the wall by the window, arms folded; his dandified clothes and easy manner a contrast to Richard's gravity, but he too had reason for discontent.

The King paused momentarily to glare at all three of his sons. 'I will not tolerate it', he shouted. 'By God's blood, I say I will not. You have your titles, your honours – do you think I am so senile I cannot rule my empire but must leave it to such whippets? Jesu, I am not yet fifty.'

Richard said sulkily, 'You made me look a fool. You gave me Aquitaine and when I ruled there, you called me back as if I were still a boy under my tutors.'

'And so you are, or should be by your behaviour. Your extravagance, your folly, have turned your mother's people against you. You have not the slightest idea how to handle men.'

'That is not so.' Eleanor spoke coldly. 'My Aquitanians love me and they will obey my son under my guidance. Richard was a little overzealous in enforcing his authority perhaps, my people are somewhat easy-going, but –'

'They are my subjects, madame,' the King retorted, 'And it is my word that is law.'

She was angry now. 'I was duchess there before I wed you, my lord.'

'And England? And Normandy?' the younger Henry demanded. 'Father, you invested me with these lands, you gave me my crown – am I to be allowed nothing?'

'You have my love and my trust.' The King paused in his furious striding. 'Isn't that enough?' He laid his hands momentarily on his eldest son's shoulders. 'You are my heir. What more do you want?'

'More than an empty title,' Henry retorted and for once did not respond to the passionate appeal. He was eighteen now and determined. 'Let me at least have Normandy – I have done homage to our suzerain for that.'

'Louis?' The King gave a contemptuous snort. 'That bumbling fool God's teeth, boy, suzerain he may be but he holds little compared to what I have under my hand. You have his daughter for wife – we need no more from him.'

'And what about *my* wife?' Richard demanded. 'When am I to have the Princess Alice and make my court at

Poitiers?'

'And mine at Rennes?' Geoffrey had a cup and ball in his hand and he threw the ball, catching it neatly. His smile was still there, though there were times when William thought he was likely to be the most dangerous of the cubs. 'Constance and I have been betrothed since we were children and now we're both fifteen we ought to have our own household in Brittany.'

The King barely glanced at him. 'You are still children and you must needs take third place, my son. As for you, Richard,' a sudden withdrawn look shadowed his eyes, 'you shall have your bride in due course – when it pleases me.'

'Pleases you!' Richard exclaimed violently, but his mother laid a hand on his sleeve and said smoothly, 'Yes, Henry, this wedding should take place and as soon as possible.'

He faced her, a bland expression on his face. 'Another year's delay will do no harm. Satisfy your lusty body elsewhere, boy.'

'It is not that,' Richard was furious. 'Just because you –' he broke off, silenced by a look this time from his brother as young Henry broke in: 'You have not answered me, my lord, and I am the eldest. Will you give me leave to go into England with my Queen?'

'You would empty the treasury in a month, squandering my gold on those greedy, landless knights who scramble to be in your train. England is better off under men I can trust.'

'You have just said you trust me,' the Young King retorted. 'With the Council to guide me –'

His father turned on him, and then seemingly became aware of William Marshal, still standing awkwardly in the doorway. 'Well, Messire Marshal, can you not teach other skills than arms? Can you not teach this boy what it means to be a ruler of men? Oh enough, enough! You may go – all of you.'

Thankfully, William escaped. His sympathies were with his young master for it seemed it would have been better not to have given him so much than to snatch it all back again, leaving the boy with no more than a hollow crown, an empty ducal coronet.

Turning a corner he almost ran into his brother. John Marshall had grown fat with the years and even more serious; he was seldom in France and when they met it was as the barest of acquaintances, but John continued to remember he was the elder brother.

'I hear your young lord continues to flout his father,' he said, puffing a little for he had just come up the stair. 'You would have done better, William, to serve the Old King. That young man will lead you into mischief.'

'From which you no doubt will extricate me for the sake of our name?'

'I?' John's eyebrows went up, his bald forehead wrinkling. He failed to see the glint of humour at the back of the grey eyes. 'Youthful folly must pay its own price. Why do you not –'

The amusement had gone from William's face. 'As you say I must pay the price of my own decisions, so keep your advice, brother. I do not need it.' He walked on.

Much later, as he waited in Henry's chamber to attend him, while two pages laid out his clothes and warmed spiced wine for him, the Young King stormed in in a fair temper.

'I'll not stand it anymore,' he burst out. 'William, it is beyond all bearing. Tomorrow I will ride to Paris, to my suzerain. He at least can grant me some rights in Normandy. You will ride with me?'

But it was hardly a question and William hesitated only for a moment. He was thinking of the day when King Henry had sent for him, entrusted him with the care of his son, not doubting his loyalty. Had he to repay that trust now with an act of rebellion? But he had set his hands between those of this golden youth whose warm smile, generosity and friendliness far outbalanced the youthful intransigence, the moments when William doubted the depth of those very qualities that were so appealing. What mattered a little extravagance, youthful high spirits? And William himself was young. 'Of course I ride,' he said. 'And your lady?'

Henry's face softened. He was deep in love with his wife, but he shook his head regretfully. 'It would attract too much attention if I were to bid her prepare to leave with me. I'll explain it to her and she can follow me later. We will ride out as if we were going to the hunt.'

What he said to her William did not know but early in the morning before half the castle was awake, he rode out with the rest of the devoted train of Henry's knights to the north and the court of the King of France.

By that evening Richard had gone too, Geoffrey beside him; other barons followed, and the next morning the Queen herself, dressed in boys' clothes that became her still girlish figure, slipped out of a postern gate and rode south towards her beloved Aquitaine.

King Henry, in bitter disappointment and savage anger, sent a body of knights after her and brought her back. He told her plainly that she had incited her sons to rebel, that her devious mind was the author of their flouting of his authority and he would have no more of it. She was sent, proud and silent a prisoner to Winchester Castle, under the charge of Ranulf de Glanville.

In Paris King Louis greeted his young son-in-law with

affection, whether simulated or not William did not know. But there was no doubting the feelings of the young Dauphin, Philip, who flung his arm about Henry's shoulders as if he were indeed a brother. They were constantly together, riding out with hawks on their wrists, shooting at the butts, playing chess, talking long and earnestly. Richard and Geoffrey were often with them and King Louis smiled on the four young men.

'I have the King of England at my side,' he boasted. 'There is no other.' And when Queen Margaret joined her husband, he promised Richard that he would command King Henry to allow his other daughter to return to Paris for their wedding. He misunderstood Richard's frown, tapping him on the shoulder and assuring him his desires would soon be fulfilled. But Sir Bertran de Born who had accompanied the Young King whispered a few words in the ear of the Dauphin. Mischief-making again, William thought, and doubted if King Henry would allow Alice to return to her father's court. Or that the Princess herself would desire it.

William enjoyed himself in Paris. He met a number of old acquaintances; his fame in arms and at the tourney had gained him a considerable name now and in a joust outside Chantilly he won a fat purse that enabled him to replenish his wardrobe. Among his companions were Robert de Barri, a young squire from Pembrokeshire who had been sent by Strongbow, his overlord, to learn his skills abroad, and Gerald de Barri his young brother, who was attending the schools in Paris, destined for holy orders, and they brought him news and greetings from his old friend.

In the evenings William danced with Queen Margaret in the great stone arched hall, as attentive to her needs as to those of his lord, and it was his pleasure to see that she had wine if she was thirsty, a girl to fetch her mantle if she grew chilly. Now he could no longer hide from himself, though he hoped it was hidden from others, that his feelings for her went deeper than those of a merely attentive member of her household. One evening, sitting beside her and watching some tumblers leaping about the rush-strewn floor, he remembered Strongbow's words when they were at Pembroke: 'It is good to have a wife, children –' But never by word or gesture could he betray this love that he had discovered in himself, and where would he find another woman to fill his eyes and his heart as she had come to do, unobtrusively, over the last years. He would rather remain unwed and he glanced at her swiftly, seeing the gentle brown eyes full of amusement at the antics of the Moorish entertainers, the mouth he would have liked to kiss but was not for him. She was unattainable and he would have to look elsewhere for a purpose in his life, and at that moment a decision came to him.

He would ask for knighthood with its oaths to chivalry and honour and these would strengthen his resolve. Determined to do it at once he made an excuse and left her and it seemed to him that she hardly noticed his going, though she gave him a quick smile, for she was clapping the tumblers, her attention all for them.

He went to his master and with permission rode to his cousin at Tancarville, the man from whom above all others he wished to receive his spurs. The Chamberlain gave his consent willingly, for he was extremely proud of William – though he would not have said so for the world – and he made arrangements for the ceremony to take place on the following Sunday.

William was invested with all due solemnity, having emptied his purse to array himself with all the necessary clothing and arms, a rich mantle of blue sendal hanging from his shoulders, his mail shirt of the finest workmanship, his helm the best he could buy. His cousin gave him spurs and a new shield bearing his arms and, making his vows, William determined that though some men might hold them lightly, a mere formality, to him they would be a lifetime's guiding principle.

Kneeling to receive the accolade he prayed he might keep his shield untarnished, his honour without stain. It gave him a new sense of purpose, a determination that would uphold him against the onslaughts of temptation, and when he rose from his knees it was as if the Hand of God had touched him on this day, as if his knighthood had made another man of him.

Unfortunately on his way back to his master he was so short of funds after his recent extravagance that he was forced to sell the new mantle. It afforded him a certain amusement – it seemed that after all some things were not changed and he parted from the mantle with regret.

On his return Henry asked that he should now be given his spurs at William's hands, saying with that spontaneous warmth so peculiarly his own, that he could not receive them from anyone worthier. How then, William thought, could he do other than serve this young King and his Queen, with his own feelings buried deep within. And because he was the man he was, he was successful in beating down those desires. There was always fighting to be done and hard riding, and he spent more time with hounds or hawks than in the palace.

He acquired a body servant, a man named Jehan whose hunched shoulder kept him from bearing arms. He spoke seldom but when he did it was to the point, and he kept his master's clothes in order and his arms polished.

Bearing a knight's banner at last – five golden billets on a tawny ground – William found the days full, yet when he lay at night in a high room on the Ile de la Cité listening to the bells of Notre Dame he could not entirely rid his mind of the image of Margaret's gentle face. It haunted him so that once or twice he flung himself from his bed and went out into the dark streets among the pimps and prostitutes, the scavengers and drunkards that made the Parisian night a hazard, to seek a woman's company. All cats were grey in the dark, he thought with rare cynicism, but these moments barely impinged on him. The truth was that his love for Margaret, so patently without hope of fulfilment, occupied his mind more than his body and no woman had yet roused the reality of passion in him.

From the French King's court Henry had sent urgent messages to England, to his friends the Earls of Leicester and Norfolk and Clare, young Gilbert de Clare, the Lords of Mowbray and Ferrars and others, to rise in his name, claim England for him. He had a seal struck and issued writs, he promised lands in England to all French nobles who would support him, including the whole of Lincolnshire to the greedy Count of Boulogne.

'Have a care, my lord,' William said. 'You have other friends in England who will want to keep what they have hazarded for you.'

'I shall make all right,' Henry said airily. 'You will see, William, I shall be such a ruler as England has never seen when we have caged the old lion.'

But the old lion was not done yet. His loyal men in England not only defeated ignominiously the army raised for the Young King, but also captured the King of Scotland who had taken the opportunity to invade the north. King Henry crossed the channel, seized the castles of the rebels and forced their submission, fining them heavily for their disloyalty. Robert de Beaumont, Earl of

Leicester, and Hugh Bigod, Earl of Norfolk, he sent to imprisonment in Falaise Castle with the Earl of Clare and his son. Then he returned to Normandy and marched against the French King.

William with his young master and the other princes was at the same time marching on Rouen, but they were still some five miles from that city when a scouting party rode in to say that King Henry was already there with a large army preparing to meet his enemies.

Louis sat in his tent, his face pale, thin fingers plucking at his beard. At last he said, 'We will return to Paris.'

'Return?' Henry asked, aghast, and Richard exclaimed, 'In God's name, why? We are a match for my father.'

'Why?' Louis gave him a weary stare. 'You do not know him if you do not see that he has outwitted us. You will get no help from England now. Our time will come – another day, another hour.' He rose and gave the order for the packing up of his tent and a general retreat. The three princes strode away together, for once in complete agreement. 'What can we do?' Henry demanded, and Geoffrey added, 'William, you heard – what can we do?'

'Nothing, my lords,' William said plainly. This time your father has won with hardy a blow struck, and you must make your peace with him – as must we all.'

When the time came they met the King at Gisors in the shade of a great oak tree, and a truce was arranged which yielded nothing to the rebellious sons. King and Duke and Count though they might be, the titles remained empty. Louis sat in his chair under the branches and accepted the terms dictated by his old enemy, by the man who had stolen his first wife and humiliated him, the King who strode up and down, still the restless, strong, dominating figure.

And when William came in turn to kneel and ask for

pardon, he received a long penetrating stare. 'Well, William Marshal? I gave my eldest son into your care. I did not look to see you foster rebellion in him.'

'Sire,' – there was no point now in dissembling even if he had been the man to do it – 'you made him my master so that my first loyalty was to him. And he has won more than that from me.' William hesitated, looking up into the hard eyes, the shadows of the leaves above traced on his long white surcoat. 'I believed his cause to be right, what else could I do but follow him?'

'To defy me? To meet me in battle if God had willed it?'

'That is true, sire, though I did not wish for it, as you must surely know. But you have dealt hardly with my master. You put a crown on his head and made it an empty bauble.'

The King's laugh was harsh. 'Would you have me give power into the hands of an inexperienced youth? It takes me all my time to keep my barons in check – including you whom I thought to trust.'

'I have not been disloyal to your son, sire.'

'And what of your loyalty to me?'

'It is vested in your son,' William said. He had a sudden memory of the miserable cell at Lusignan where he had lain for so long, and wondered if he was to be sent to Falaise to join the other rebels. If so, he must do what he could for his young master first. 'My lord,' he went on urgently, 'deal with me as you will, but give your son work to do. He is only idle and frivolous because he has no responsibility. If you are reconciled to him, if you allow him to rule at least in part, I would not stand at the crossroads.'

'Christ's wounds!' the King swore, 'you are bold, William.'

'I think, sire, because I have little left to lose.'

There was a moment's silence. Then the King held out the hilt of his sword. 'Well, I'll not condemn you for loving my son, but it is not yet time, nor am I in my dotage. Will you renew your fealty?'

William set his hand on the cross-piece. 'To you, sire, and to your son, my master.'

'Jesu!' Henry said, 'you are as bad as they are! Please God, you've all learned your lesson.'

At that the young Dauphin sprang forward from his place behind his father's chair. 'You have humiliated us all,' he cried out, his fair skin flushed with anger. 'You think you have won all, but when I am a man, by God, I will take back all you've taken from us.'

The King threw back his head and laughed. 'Listen to the bantam crowing! You are not cock of the yard yet, my fine prince.' He stared round the opposing circle of faces, seeing the angry youth, Louis pale and disillusioned, the French lords humiliated, his own sons shamed, and he turned on his heel and left them.

Much later in the tent the young princes shared, Henry turned to William and tears of rage and frustration ran down his face. 'I hate him!' He could scarcely get the words out 'Oh God, I hate him! He is a devil – a devil.'

'My dear lord,' William said, 'it is not thus you should think of him. He is your father and he has been generous to us. We have our freedom.'

Richard, who had been leaning silently against the tent pole, his arms folded, gave a sudden snort. 'Do you not know, William, we are the children of Melusine? From the devil we came, so it is hardly surprising that the devil should strive with us.'

It was the second time that day that William had remembered Lusignan, the seat of that legend of Melusine, and he turned now on the younger prince in rare annoyance. 'That is small comfort to my lord, saving your grace's pardon. The best must be made of a bad business.' He poured wine and gave it into the Young King's hand. 'Drink this, my lord. Of one thing I am sure. Your father loves you dearly –'

'A strange sort of love,' Geoffrey retorted. 'We are no better off than before – worse, for he will be even less willing to yield one acre of land to us.'

Henry raised reddened eyes from the cup of wine. Then with his other hand he seized William's arm. 'I wish I understood why. But stay by me, William. He did not dismiss you, so don't leave me.'

William sat down beside him on the pallet. 'As long as I have life in me, I will never leave you – unless you send me away. And when you are King indeed –'

Richard precipitated himself from the tent pole, 'When lions learn to fly!' he retorted and stalked out of the tent.

So the quarrel ended for the time being, but it soon flared up again. When King Louis died his son Philip began sowing further dissension among the devil's brood, and there was seldom any lasting peace. At one moment Richard fought his father, angered at the permanent imprisonment of his mother, and Henry aided him; at another Henry fought Richard, siding with his father. Geoffrey defied the old King and nearly killed him with a quarrel fired from the walls of his castle at Rennes, and only John, growing into dark lanky boyhood, remained with the King. Richard was the most intransigent of all, the most obstinate.

'Richard yea and nay,' Bertran de Born sang mockingly. 'Oh fairest Richard, we know you well, if you say yea, your word is given; if 'tis nay, 'tis very hell – you will not change your mind.'

'Dear God,' William said, 'deliver us from poets!'

CHAPTER FIVE

Richard Strongbow was dead and his only daughter Isabel became a ward at King Henry's court where, at Chinon in the Christmas of 1182, William saw her for the first time. She was nine years old and he came upon her the day after he and his master had ridden in for Christmas.

She was sitting in the ladies' bower when he came in with a message for Queen Margaret from her husband, and he was struck at once by the child's likeness to her father. She had the same fair hair, the same eyes set slantwise, and her smile reminded him of Strongbow that day at Boulogne when he had lost his horse.

Isabel answered his greeting shyly and he sat down beside her and talked to her for a little while. He had grieved for his friend, dying from a fever caught in the marshes of Ireland, and he was sorry for this lonely child whose mother had died in childbirth. She did not remember her father either, for she had been no more than three years old when he had succumbed to the fever, and William told her of their first meeting and how he had won Strongbow's horse and given it back and how in the turmoil of the King's arrival at Pembroke the debt had never been paid.

Isabel listened rapt to the tale and when he had finished she said, 'The best gift is the one we receive when we need it most, is it not, messire? My father must have thought it so even though you did not get your horse.'

William glanced at her, surprised at her perception, and she added, her cheeks a deeper pink, 'I must take the debt upon myself, messire.'

He laughed and took her hand. 'Child, I did not tell you the story for that reason. Your father's friendship was enough return.'

Over her head he looked at Margaret who was smiling too. 'She is a good child,' the Queen said, 'and I am glad to have her with me.' After a moment she added, 'It is the first time we have all been together for Christmas for so long. Is it not good, William, that King Henry and his sons are reconciled at last?'

'Very good, madame,' he agreed and honesty compelled him to add, 'I pray that it may last.'

She gave a little sigh. 'There are other things too that I pray for – that might bring even greater peace.'

And I, he thought, but he understood what she meant. She was twenty-five years old now and had borne her husband only one child who had died at birth – young enough still to hope but it was nevertheless an abiding sorrow, colouring the last few years. These had been spent by William riding about Europe in his lord's train and something subtle had entered into their relationship that disturbed him. But for the moment he was not thinking of that. As always when he was with Margaret his thoughts were all for her and he was glad Princess Alice was not in the room. Duke Richard still waited for his bride; Alice looked mockingly at him and slid away from him. The old King might think that no one knew of his liaison with her but the truth was that everyone down to the lowest scullion knew, and William was sorry for Margaret who must bear some part of her sister's shame.

His love for her had not changed in all the years but he was content now merely to serve her and he knew he had at least her warm affection. It was a small reward for all the self-repression he had had to exercise. Women there had been but only of the tavern or the brothel, taken as any man might for a brief hour of sensual pleasure. They meant nothing to him and were as quickly forgotten and, absorbed in his concern for Margaret's comfort on their travels, he failed to notice his lord's occasional quick frown. He had been with Henry so long that he did not think to question their relationship.

Seeing the sadness in her face he said, 'Your grace, I'm sure heaven will answer the prayers of one so good.'

'Am I good?' she queried, half humorously though the sadness lingered. 'All I know is that I would bear my lord a son and that I have not done. Isabel, dear child, pray fetch me a fresh skein of silk, I have no more of this green.'

The girl jumped up with a quick smile for the man who had been her father's friend and when she had gone Margaret went on, 'Tell me, William, do you think my lord has changed? Since you came back from Germany, he has seemed – I don't know – as if some secret thing is eating at him. Or perhaps it is only the old trouble, that King Henry treats him as if he were a boy. He is twenty-six and is no nearer ruling his lands than ever he was.'

William did not answer immediately. He looked at the embroidery in her hands and saw that she was stitching at a panel showing her husband's favourite badge, an ermine in the centre supported by two sprigs of the *planta genesta,* the wild broom, the colours gold and white and green artistically blended.

She was right, he thought, Henry had changed. The old friendship between them was still there on the surface but something new was creeping into it. Small incidents rankled, such as that awkward occasion not long ago in Flanders when the Queen was not with them. They were in a small town for a tourney and short of money as usual, the boxes of coin from England delayed, and Henry could not pay the Flemish innkeepers for all the food and drink consumed by his large household. As usual he had been generous, ordering only the best of everything for his friends, many of whom William considered mere spongers. The burgesses of the town had the gates closed and refused to let them leave until the debt should be paid, nor would they accept the Young King's assurances. William had stepped in and pledged the money, promising to win enough and more at the joust the next day, and they accepted his word at once. A black frown settled on Henry's face and Bertran de Born raised an amused eyebrow remarking, 'What fellows they are, to take a knight's pledge before yours, my lord. But I suppose we should all bow to William – as King of the tourney!' which remark did nothing to mollify Henry.

Randulph de Blundevill, who had lately succeeded his father as Earl of Chester and had joined the Young King's train, said, 'God's blood. I'd not tolerate their impertinence sire. Have one of the fellows whipped – the sight of flayed flesh will soon bring them to their senses.'

'Foolish advice, my lord,' William interrupted sharply, and saw the Earl's face suffuse with angry colour. De Blundevill had not been long enough in Henry's train to understand the particular place occupied by one whom he considered below him in rank, and he was furious at being thus reproved. Unperturbed, William went on, 'Do you want our master's name to be besmirched by such dealings?'

Henry's Seneschal, a knight with a proud and disdainful manner whom William had never liked, ranged himself on the new Earl's side, adding with a touch of sarcasm in his voice, 'You must understand, my lord of Chester, that Sir William considers himself the guardian of our knightly principles.'

'Oh, have done,' William said curtly. 'I have said the money will be paid and there's an end of it.'

But it was not the end of the matter, for at the joust the next day the assembled lords and knights who had ridden in from considerable distances vied with each other to fight the Marshal, as they called him, though his brother still held that office in England. The Young King was almost ignored. He was a good horseman, though not brilliant. He had studied all William had taught him, how to use his heaume and lance, how to judge the best moment to strike, to keep his destrier under control, when to use the ball and spike spur he had adopted, but he did not excel as his brother Richard did, and he could not hope to emulate William.

William won as usual and the townsfolk received their monies, but the affair rankled. And there were those in Henry's train who were openly jealous. The Earl of Chester, in William's opinion, indulged a cruel streak above average in their tough world, and he began to lead the Young King into wild excesses, taking pleasure in flouting William's more sober advice. On one occasion, in a fit of fury at his lack of recognition and the miserable shortage of money, Henry allowed himself to be talked by de Blundevill into raiding an abbey just over the border into Normandy and seizing all the gold and silver they could lay their hands on to sell in the markets of Paris. And when William remonstrated Henry retorted that the fat monks owed him dues in any case, while de Bora told the Marshal he was becoming tiresomely moral.

William said no more. It seemed to him that his very fame was bringing its price in the envy of other men. He was besieged by young sprigs wanting to squire him, by fathers willing to pay for their sons to be taught the knightly arts, and while he cared little for the opinion of such men as de Blundevill and de Born, if it should alienate the master he had now served so devotedly for twelve years he would willingly throw it all away. 'Pay no heed to them,' Gilbert de Clare advised. He had long been released from Falaise Castle. 'You have more friends than enemies, William.'

He hoped it was so, but it was Henry's friendship that he cared for most. When, with King Philip of France, Henry took the Cross, determined to go to the Holy Land to fight against the Moslem leader Sallah-ed-din, at the same time failing to ask William to take it with him, he began to have his doubts.

He hoped this Christmas gathering would heal the rift, settle the quarrels between the brothers and their father, but again he had his doubts. However there was always hope for there had not been such a meeting for many years. The Princess Matilda had come with her husband Duke Henry of Saxony, and their two small boys who ran wild in the great castle, encouraged by fourteen-year-old Prince John to get into mischief far beyond their years. They all hung about William, begging him to show them how to use sword and spear, and he thought privately that John, growing up with all the family good looks but the dark colouring of his mother, was showing signs of an unpleasantly vicious nature. He made sport with his dogs until they yelped with pain; once he had hung up a lymer hound by the leg until it died, because it had disobeyed a command. His pages often bore the weal of a whip on their cheeks and once it was whispered that he had forced one to hold a hand over the candle flame until it blistered because he had spilt a little wine on one of John's rich pelisses. John attended to no one, except perhaps his brother Count Geoffrey, but in his father's eyes he could do no wrong. Geoffrey's wife was also there, Constance of the sharp tongue. It was the Princess Joanna, far away in Sicily with her husband, whose presence, William felt, would have done much to help the reconciliation, particularly as she exerted the most influence over the obstinate Richard.

As far as Queen Eleanor was concerned the old King would not yield. He could forgive his sons over and over again, but not their mother, nor her fierce upholding of her adored Richard, and he could not, or would not, see that Richard would never be at peace with him until she was at liberty.

One morning Richard had said abruptly, 'Come out with me to the practice field, William Marshal, and let us try our skills together.'

For a solid hour they battered at each other before agreeing to call a halt. Richard had phenomenal strength and whatever William might think of his behaviour off the field, he could not but admire the Duke's handling of his weapons, his talent as a soldier and a leader of knights, and he said so.

Richard's rare smile came. 'And I admire the love and loyalty I know you feel for my mother,' he said frankly. That is why I asked you out here this morning – to tell you so. I will not forget that.'

Was the Duke trying to bid for loyalty to his own cause too, William wondered? Yet Richard must know that he had one master whom he put first – but it was always there, the contention over Queen Eleanor. Henry too resented the continued absence of his mother and could scarcely bring himself to speak to Princess Alice.

Now William gave a heavy sigh and in answer to Queen Margaret's question he said, 'Yes, lady, he has changed and I am sorry if it saddens you. But so much has changed.'

'I know.' She laid a hand briefly on his arm. 'Dear William, we have never had in our household anyone as devoted as you and if my lord is out of temper you will forgive him – for my sake? I have my own sorrows.'

'For your sake,' William agreed and put her fingers to his lips. After all these years the desire to take her in his arms and comfort her rose once again so that he stood up abruptly, shaken by sudden emotion. And as he turned towards the door he saw Henry standing there, one hand on the curtain, an expression on the freckled handsome face that William had never before seen directed at him.

Two days after the Christmas feast William's enemies struck. He never knew how it came about but he was summoned to the Old King's presence to find his master there, with the Earl of Chester, Sir Bertran de Born, and the Seneschal.

The Old King, his red hair turning grey now, his skin mottled with tiny veins, was seated on the side of his great bed while his page pulled on his hunting boots. He looked up as William entered, waited until the boy had finished before dismissing him with a mild kick. Then he stood up.

'Well, Sir William –' his tone was harsher than usual, '– it seems you have exceeded the commission we gave you and in a manner unbecoming to one of your station.'

William stood rooted in the doorway, utterly taken aback. It was the first time either King Henry or his son had ever reminded him of what he remained, a plain knight without possessions, and seeing the amusement on de Born's face, the grim satisfaction in that of the Earl of Chester, the cold disdain of the Seneschal, he felt his colour rise but he answered as calmly as usual. 'In what way, sire?'

'I am told that because you excel in arms you put yourself above my son; that he, who should receive the highest attention on the field, takes second place to you, that your word is taken before his, that you seek your fame at the expense of his.'

'Who accuses me of these things?' William demanded. He glanced at his master but Henry was staring sulkily at the floor. William turned back to look directly at the King. 'To answer the first, sire, it is not by my will that other knights clamour to challenge me, but if they do so I cannot turn my back on them.'

'You've become so puffed up you look to be the hero of every joust,' the Earl of Chester interposed. 'As for the young fools who flock round you every time you enter the lists –' he gave a coarse laugh but was silenced by one glance from the Old King.

'It is not only Sir William who is puffed up, my lord of Chester. But there seems to be some truth in these accusations, William. I have heard tales that I cannot like, that I find hard to believe of you.'

Henry raised his head at that, his blue eyes stormy, his mouth petulant. 'You shamed me in Flanders! You were my tutor once but by Our Lady I am no yellowbeak now, and I will not be put out of countenance by a mere knight and a landless one at that.'

His words astounded William. He braced himself and retorted, 'I thought that business in Flanders rankled with you, but what was I to do? They would not let us go with our debts unpaid.'

Henry's face was scarlet 'They would have heeded me – in time – if you hadn't interfered.'

'Interfered! Sire, may I remind you that I gave you, willingly, all my prizes to pay our score.'

'No, you may not! It was your duty, your sworn duty to aid your lord.'

If it had not been so grave a matter William could have

laughed at the contradictoriness of this statement, but as it was he did not know how to answer. It seemed to him there was no real accusation to answer, that the charges were concocted by men whom he had long suspected of being jealous of his position, whom he knew now for his enemies in earnest. He addressed himself to the Old King. 'Sire, surely you must see that I have done no more than serve your son as you bade me do so many years ago. If I have some skill in arms –' he ignored a snort from de Blundevill '– am I not to use it? If I had the means to aid my master who was without money, should I not have done so? And, his determination to vindicate himself got the better of his judgement, 'your son was without gold in his purse because he had not received his just dues as either King of England or Duke of Normandy.'

At this unwise speech, the Old King reared his head. 'You dare to bring me to book? God's bones, William Marshal, you go too far. I see now why my son's attendants complain of you. Would you rule us all – you, without one virgate of land to call your own?'

Stiffly William bowed. 'Your pardon, sire. Perhaps I should not have said what I did. The truth is often unpalatable.'

There was a slight gasp from de Born who glanced at the Old King to see what he would say next, for his temper was rising.

'And you think that because it is the truth you may say what you will to me?' The King gave a hard laugh. 'You put me in mind of Thomas Becket in his most infuriating mood. I tell you, you will know who is King and who is not while I live.'

'I set my hands between yours before ever I set them between your son's, sire. That gave my allegiance to you both and now I am in straits to please you both.'

Sir Bertran made the King a courtly bow. 'Your grace. Sir William would have us believe his motives are of the most noble and therefore the masters he serves must be of less noble mind to call him to account. But this cannot be. I think I shall write a *sirventes* on the subject of overweening pride.'

'This is no joking matter,' the Young King's Seneschal said in his thin sharp voice, but he received only a mocking glance from de Born.

'Do you think I'm not in earnest? Pride is one of the deadly sins – or so the churchmen tell us.'

'In God's name!' William broke in. 'My honour has been impugned and you make play with it. Sire, give me leave to challenge any or all of these knights to single combat and defend my honour with my body.'

At that de Born broke into open laughter. 'Oh easy, easy! You know you can beat us all in the field. And if you carry a lady's colours –' he broke off, as if he said too much, but the words were deliberate.

'What are you saying?' William demanded. 'I have not the least idea of what you mean.'

'You have, you have, and so have I!' The Young King who had been standing, legs straddled, before the fire set deep in a hearth in the castle wall, strode forward to stand beside his father, seizing hold of one of the bed posts. 'Do you think I don't know that you look with desire at my lady? Do you think I have not seen you linger over her hand, seek her company more than is needful – we all have. My lord,' he looked down at his father, still seated on the bed, 'ask Sir Bertran, ask Randulph, ask the Seneschal of my household, who pays most attention to the Queen – more than is proper. They will tell you –'

William had stepped backwards involuntarily. The utter unexpectedness of this last attack stunned him. After all the years of repression, of hiding his love, doing no more than serve the Young Queen with perhaps more concern than some for her daily welfare, to be accused of lusting after her brought a dark flush of bitter resentment to his face. And the cruelty, the injustice of it, brought out not only before the King, but in the face of these other men, lesser men at least in years of loyal service, galled him beyond measure. In that instant he saw how blind he had been not to see that Henry was jealous.

'You lie, sir,' he said at last, 'and you must know it.'

'I do not,' Henry retorted, too angry now to retreat. 'And you dare to call your lord a liar! I want no more of you.'

'One moment my son.' The Old King rose and stood in silence, looking at the tall rigid figure in a plain soldier's mantle, the amethyst brooch fastening it – and though he had not thought of it for years a sudden memory came to him, the memory of how and where William had received that clasp. It was as if now it was flaunted before him, as if the treasured gift spoke of yet another loyalty, to an imprisoned Queen whom he thought of as the initial cause of all his troubles. It turned his judgement finally against William.

'Well,' he barked. 'I will have the truth of this at least. Have you dared to love Queen Margaret, have you lusted after her? If so, you are the most loathsome of servants, one who would cuckold his master.'

William thought of the Princess Alice and this angry man slipping secretly along the corridors to her bedchamber, cuckolding his own son. But this time caution prevailed; if he valued his life he must not allude to that. Yet neither could he wholly deny his love. Quietly and with dignity, he said, 'If I have thought of the Queen with love it has been as one who serves. I have done no more than care for her comfort, no more than –'

'Oh!' The Young King clenched his hands. 'I have seen you –'

'You have seen me do nothing dishonourable,' William retorted and suddenly his calmness deserted him and the pent-up anger, the desire for justification, blazed up against the base accusations, the ingratitude of this young man who had been his friend, to whom he had given unstintingly twelve years of service. How could he believe what he was saying? 'You all accuse me,' he said hotly, 'yet you will not allow me to defend myself as knighthood permits. I deny every charge, the last most of all. What more can I do?'

'God's Bones, you have done enough,' the Old King said with finality. 'When my daughter-in-law's name is brought into it, it is time to end the matter. I am going out with my hawks now; I do not expect to find you here when I return, Sir William.'

William gave one last look at the fiery, petulant and oddly defiant face of his master, but Henry stared back unrelentingly. Master he was no more and William, hurt, bewildered and bitterly angry, turned and left the room.

He went out of the royal apartments down the stair into the hall. Men were gathered there ready for the hunt, women sitting in groups with their sewing or playing with the younger children, dogs lay by the fire or scuffed in the rushes. There was all the usual noise and busyness but William strode through it, ignoring a call from one friend, a casual remark from another. Out in the courtyard he stood, drawing deep breaths of fresh cold air, his head reeling, still unable to believe that he, William Marshal, champion of Europe, friend of the Young King, had been dismissed on the word of a few envious men. And who had first sown the seeds of doubt? The face of de Born came before him and he ground his teeth in rare fury, his pride in shreds. Bertran had always desired his place in the younger Henry's affections, he knew that, but he had never thought of him as a rival. Now de Born and the others had won and he wished he had them facing him in the field.

But he must go, get away from this place – only where should he go? And suddenly it seemed to him that because he had loved where he had no right to love he had in that at least been at fault. Before he went back to the old life of tourneys and living by his sword he would go on pilgrimage – somewhere, anywhere – to ease his conscience. The memory of the last half-hour's humiliation must be erased somehow, and if he offered his penance to God perhaps some good might in the end come out of it all.

He wished that Will FitzHenry was here so that he might talk to him, for of all his friends Will was the most sensitive to the needs of others. The knights he spent his time with were tough, hard-riding men who lived in the saddle and had little time for the niceties of life and there was no one in whom he could confide. But Will was in England with his brother Geoffrey, now King Henry's Chancellor. Only Will perhaps would have understood why he wanted to go on this pilgrimage.

And he could not even take farewell of his mistress, for Henry in his present mood would make sure William had no access to the Queen's apartments. His face burned again; the injustice of it was a hurt that would not easily heal. He wanted one more sight of Margaret's face but perhaps it was as well that he could not have it for he might not have been able to command himself under this burden of misunderstanding.

Aware once more of a deep loneliness, of Richard Strongbow's words of long ago, he went heavily to his chamber to order the stolid Jehan to pack his possessions into saddle bags, but when he got there he found a stern-looking young clerk awaiting him and a lad of about fifteen, a dark youth with a slightly twisted mouth and thin hands clasped tightly together. If William had not been so torn by the wretchedness of the scene he had just endured he might have seen the nervous eagerness, the anxiety in the boy's face. As it was he was in no mood for importunate strangers and asked curtly what they wanted.

The clerk said stiffly, 'I ask your pardon if we have come at an inconvenient moment, Sir William. I am Hubert Walter, chaplain to my uncle Sir Ranulf de Glanville and –'

'To Sir Ranulf?' William interrupted, momentarily deflected from his own affairs. Then you can tell me: Queen Eleanor, is she well treated? I had heard so, but –'

'It is true,' the clerk answered in precise tones. 'My uncle is her gaoler and watches over her most carefully, but she has pleasant quarters and much freedom for her household. This lad here has been her page.'

William turned to look at the boy for the first time. 'Why have you left her service, then?' And his voice was harsher than he realised so that the lad flushed.

'She says that now I am fifteen I must be a squire and she sent me to you. She said you would remember her kindly.' William's annoyance died, the emotions of the last hour simmering still but below the surface. How should he not remember Eleanor of Aquitaine kindly? 'I owe that lady more than I can ever repay,' he said at last. 'My life perhaps. I would do anything she asked of me but I am leaving Caen at once, so you had best seek another master.'

If Hubert Walter was surprised he did not show it 'The Queen told him to seek no other. Will you not take him,

Sir William?'

'I cannot offer explanations at the moment but the fact is that I am no longer in a position to do so. I am going to Flanders, to Germany perhaps, but out of King Henry's realm, and I must dismiss the squires I have, not take another.'

This time Hubert Walter expressed his astonishment. 'I grieve to hear this. I thought – but it is not my affair. Only I wish you your place again. As for this lad –'

'Oh, please, messire,' the boy broke in, 'let me come with you. I'll do anything you wish – you will need a body servant –'

'I have one,' William said with finality and put up a hand to unfasten his mantle. His fingers touched the amethyst clasp and he thought of Eleanor as she had been that day at Boulogne, beautiful, gracious, and he wondered how the years of imprisonment had dealt with her. She had saved him from a worse fate, 'What is your name, boy?' he asked abruptly.

'John d'Erleigh, messire.'

'Then, John d'Erleigh, get your gear if you wish to come with me for I'll waste no more time. I can't promise you much, only enough to eat and what skills I can teach you.'

The lad's face was alight and even the solemn Hubert Walter added an austere expression of gratitude.

An hour later, attended only by his new squire and Jehan leading a pack mule, he rode under the barbican and out of the castle. He did not see Isabel at a high window wave her hand to him, nor Queen Margaret standing behind, her eyes full of tears.

CHAPTER SIX

Gilbert de Clare had married a wife, one of the heiresses of the late Earl of Gloucester, and having got her with child within two months of their wedding, considered himself free for the moment to follow his own pursuits. He left her at Clare in Suffolk in the charge of his mother and returned to Normandy to rejoin the Young King where he was horrified to hear what had happened in his absence. He spoke his mind in no uncertain terms and it was perhaps owing to this that he was on a particular mission on a cold day in January. He arrived at nightfall, making his way through softly falling snow to an inn, the only inn at Noyon, where he was told he would find the man he was seeking.

William was eating his supper with his squire, mopping up the juices of the meat with pieces of manchet bread. Glancing up, he was astonished to see Gilbert making his way round a noisy table of young men. He sprang up.

'What in God's name are you doing here? I thought you at home with your bride – are you tired already of the marriage bed?'

Gilbert gave him a swift grin. 'Amicia is with child. She complains that she feels unwell and my mother fusses over her. I have done my share of the business for the moment and hope I've got a boy under her kirtle.'

'Lusty fellow,' William said. He poured a cup of wine for Gilbert and sent John d'Erleigh to order more food and take his own plate elsewhere. 'But you have not said what brings you to this out-of-the-way place.'

'You,' Gilbert answered cryptically. He threw off his mantle and sat down, his tunic slit to the knees as he spread his legs wide towards the fire. He took the cup and drank, his close-set eyes surveying his friend.

Sudden hope flared in William but was as quickly

repressed, none of it betrayed in his face. 'You must have heard what happened at the Christmas feast, even though you were not there at the time.'

'Yes, I heard.'

'It was none of my doing. The accusations were false.'

'I know that. We've not been friends these many years for me not to know that.'

William's mouth tightened and he pushed his plate away with no desire now to finish the meal. 'It seems others did not who should have done so.'

Gilbert for his part was eating busily, being a man who put first things first, and he was cold and hungry. Presently he said. There was a rare hornet's nest there when I did arrive – the day after you left.'

'Oh? I did not think –'

Gilbert gave him another grin, showing small sharp teeth, two missing from an unfortunate encounter with a lance.

'Not about your affairs. The cubs were at it again'. He stuffed the last gobbet of meat into his mouth and gave a satisfied belch. 'Did you not think they would be? The Old King wanted to make peace, but by Jesu he should know now how not to do it. He would have Richard do homage to our master which Richard would not, so he left for Aquitaine in a rare temper; then Geoffrey marched out because he is not to be allowed a free hand in Brittany for all he's wed at last to the lady Constance, and he had to wait long enough for that. As for John – did you know he's to marry my wife's sister?'

'No – I'd not heard that.'

'Well, It seems the Old King wants John Lackland to lose the nickname he gave him. He's to have Gloucester in Avice's right, and Nottingham and all of Cornwall as well, beside being lord of Ireland.'

'Henry won't like that. He has always thought lands in

England should be his gift, but when England has two kings –', William gave an expressive shrug.

Gilbert rubbed his chin dubiously. 'It's a great match for Avice, but whether she'll like it I can't say – not that that has anything to do with it, and the wedding won't take place yet in any case. Oh, we had a fine Twelfth Night of it, I can assure you, with the King glowering at us all, and the Princess Matilda in tears because Richard and Geoffrey had gone, and John playing the fool while de Born sang a song beseeching us to weep for "the poor prisoner" and even the thickheads could not fail to know who that was meant to be. You were well out of it, William.' He shouted to the innkeeper for more wine and then went on, 'The Old King gave John several castles in Normandy as well – as if that would not stir the pot – and our master took a cool leave of his father, I can tell you.'

He paused for breath and then suddenly asked his companion if he knew there was to be a tournament at Gournai.

'Yes, but I'm on my way to Cologne and I don't want to go back even to win a purse or two,' William answered in surprise at the change of topic. He had been listening as one who listens to a familiar tale. 'Why? Are you to fight there?'

'Yes, but that's neither here nor there. Our master –'

'He is no longer mine – by his own will. Unless,' William looked up sharply, trying to read his companion's face in the light of a flickering rush dip set in a sconce behind them, 'You have a message from him?'

'I have, but not one you will like. He is to fight at Gournai tomorrow but he has no knights with him likely to be a match for the French champion who is to be on the other side.'

'Renault de Nevers? He has great skill.'

'So we all know. Henry sent me to bid you join him tomorrow. He says your duty binds you to do so.'

'And – ?'

'That is all. God's teeth, this wine is poor stuff,' Gilbert wiped his mouth with the edge of his sleeve, the jug nevertheless empty.

There was a silence. William stared unseeingly over Gilbert's head at the busy room, the rushlight flickering on faces warmed by wine and hot food, merchants talking business, knights and squires, burgesses and apprentices, all seeking an evening's entertainment out of the cold streets. At last he said, 'No word of friendship?'

'None. I told him they lied – all of them – but he is still angry, William.'

'Without cause.'

'Will you go?'

Again William hesitated. Then he said, 'I am not bound by my word, since he dismissed me. But I will go tomorrow. After that – no more until he sends in better terms.'

In the morning he rode back with Gilbert along the road he had taken yesterday, but by the time they reached Gournai the tourney had already begun. The field was alive with mounted men, the wicker lists set up, crowds of people watching, the pennons flying in the icy January wind. William was already wearing his mail and he pulled the hood over his head, taking shield and lance from his squire. But before he bent to have his helm buckled on his eyes raked the field, and he drew a deep breath, pursing his lips.

It seemed Henry had ignored his oft-given advice, to wait before plunging into the mêlée until some of his opponents were weary. It was as if Henry had suddenly determined to assert himself, to prove after all he did not need the Marshal at his side, but he was being hard pressed. William could see the figure in the familiar armour and wearing the golden helm almost surrounded by French knights and in danger of becoming a prize himself. An assailant aimed a blow on the dazzling helm and the Young King reeled in the saddle.

William swore under his breath and setting spurs to his destrier galloped into the fight without waiting for his own helm. He was aware suddenly of sheer physical relief, that he could vent all his frustration, his bitterness, against unknown adversaries, and such was his fury that in a few moments he had carved his way to the Young King's side. There he drove off two knights without difficulty, breaking his lance against the shield of another. Then as a rider bearing a well known blazon turned on him he leaned forward and seized him by the sword belt. With one heave, using all his strength, he threw Renault de Nevers bodily from his saddle and grabbing the bridle of the riderless horse flung it to Gilbert who had followed him into the fight. Then, turning his own destrier's head he placed himself between Henry and the enemy and got him out of the fight to the safety of the lists.

There he dismounted and with grim satisfaction saw de Nevers struggling to his feet and limping off the field in the opposite direction. He waited, leaning on his saddle, while two squires helped their royal master from his war horse. Henry was dazed and as his helm was eased from his head it revealed a face drenched with sweat. The blue eyes were resentful – perhaps, contrarily, even more resentful than they would have been if he had been taken by the French champion, for his debt to William was only increased, his own behaviour proved even more base.

There was no word of thanks, no sign of gratitude, only silence, and without speaking William turned and left him.

For six months he heard no more. He rode to Cologne and laid his sword on the altar of the shrine of the Three Kings, beseeching the prayers of the Magi who had laid their own offering at the feet of Christ Himself. He confessed his sins, asking pardon for his unlawful love, and afterwards knelt with his hands clasped on the hilt of his sword, the point resting on the floor, bareheaded, his eyes fixed on the jewelled shrine. He prayed then for his young master – the end of years of friendship was bitter to him, as was the loss of the Old King's trust – and he asked that he might be able to forgive in order to be forgiven himself. Jesu, he thought, was it hard to forgive Judas?

When he left the cathedral it was to return to his old life of winning his bread by his right arm, only now it all came easily enough. And such was his popularity that he could have taken service with any lord in Europe; even the great Frederick Barbarossa sent to him, offering him a place at his side.

Yet he refused them all. John d'Erleigh, very much in awe of his new master, asked, 'Why do we not go to one of these great lords, master? You could live in greater comfort and become very rich,' while Jehan, with more familiarity, said dryly, 'You do not know us yet, boy. Our master is like a travelling minstrel, only he uses his sword instead of a string of foolish words.'

William was aware that he was waiting, and would wait longer. He could not believe that Henry had forgotten all the years of their friendship, that on reflection he would not see the baseness of the accusations, especially the last, the final insult. And surely if Henry knew anything about women he must know that his Queen loved him and no one else.

He was not blind and never had been to Henry's faults, yet there was that in him that drew men to him, William most of all, and he listened with growing anxiety to the news that came from chapmen and merchants and travelling knights. In all the years since his imprisonment at Lusignan William had never been so far from this family to whom he had given his love and his allegiance and when a serious war flared up between them all he longed to be back by the Young King's side. It seemed that Richard had defied his father, that the Old King had sent Henry and Geoffrey against him and then, inexplicably, had evened the odds by joining Richard himself. Now two warred against two, the Young King and Geoffrey holding Limoges against the forces of their father and brother. A miserable situation, and William heard that Geoffrey had unleashed all the natural violence that hid under so affable an exterior, terrorising the countryside around; that even his one-time master was raiding and plundering in a manner far exceeding what William felt a knight was entitled to do, even in war. He wished he was there to restrain Henry, to hold in check the barons like the Earl of Chester, whom he so distrusted. Yet without a summons he would not move.

It came at last. On a June evening when he was at Amiens, staying with a knight who had been pleased to offer hospitality to the famous champion, a dusty messenger rode in. He bore a ring from the Young King and a request – not a command – that Sir William Marshal would ride at once to Limoges to join him.

William stood up, the ring, always a token of love, lying in his palm. 'I will come at once,' he said and took leave of his host. It was as if a heaviness of heart, an invisible burden, had been lifted from him.

He obtained a safe conduct from King Philip of France

who regarded him with a bland expression that hid, as William knew, a calculating mind. 'You swear that you ride to aid my brother-in-law? Your quarrel is mended?' And he added, 'I never thought you guilty of any of the accusations.'

William did not like Philip, but the King's consistent care for his sister Margaret made his vindication something to be desired, and he rode freely through France until he turned south-west towards Limoges. Some miles from the city he was told that King Henry and Duke Richard lay outside it but with insufficient men to blockade it entirely, and that the young King had evaded the siege and ridden out to meet the Count of Toulouse, hoping to persuade him to take his side in the argument. William took the road to Martel and there found his old gaoler, the Count of Lusignan, nursing a broken leg. 'Damned horse threw me,' he grumbled. 'Well, William Marshal, I am glad you are come. It was I who told Henry to send for you.'

'You?' William queried in astonishment. He had met the Count at court several times in the last years but without much civility on either side. 'In God's name, why?'

The Count shifted uncomfortably. His leg had been set by the infirmarian from a nearby Priory whom he cursed for a clumsy oaf and it was hurting him excessively. The thought that he might never ride again did not improve his temper, 'Aye,' he said irritably. 'Your master and Count Geoffrey are raiding the whole countryside – well, they must pay their *routiers* I suppose, bloody thieving scum – but they need better knights to do their business. It seemed to me that Henry had more need of you than any other.'

'Why do you call him my master? It was by his own wish that I ceased to be that.'

'The more fool him,' the Count growled unexpectedly. 'I

little knew what sort of fellow I had in my tower all those years ago. Well, Henry is in a bad case. I like him, God knows why, but I swear the devil is uppermost in him now. He'll not heed any of us, but he might listen to you.'

'Where is he?' William asked quietly.

'He rode off for Rocamadour. Geoffrey had other fish to fry.'

A cold feeling of apprehension seized William. 'Rocamadour? You cannot mean – he'll not desecrate that place?'

The Count shrugged and caused himself to wince. 'God knows – and if He does His anger will be terrible. Get you there, William Marshal, and do what you can.'

Without delay William left him and rode for the holy village housing the shrine of St Amadour and its greatest treasure, the sword once used by Roland at the famous pass of Roncesvalles. Holy Saints, he thought, what madness has seized him now that he must plunder such places?

Knowing the way well, he paused only once to rest the horses and at last, with John and Jehan beside him, breasted the rise above the village. The smell of smoke had reached them before ever they looked down into the valley and now they saw several poor huts burning, thatched houses catching the flames while men-at-arms rode up and down the narrow street searching for plunder. Women were screaming, children running wildly – a scene William had viewed many times before in the necessity of war, but today a great horror filled him. This was more than a raid in a campaign that was like a game of chess, this was a holy place and the man who desecrated it offended God.

He drew his sword and rode down the stony track, leaving Jehan with the pack animal and taking only John with him, 'Keep close to me,' he said sharply, and within minutes they were in the village. Almost at once he had to draw his horse back on its haunches as a shrieking child ran from a burning house, the flames already at her dress. Before he could dismount, John was off his horse and had beaten at the fire but the girl fled from him in terror and a beam collapsed on her. A man with a bleeding stump where an arm had been ran out of an alley and screamed abuse at them. William leaned down and caught him by the collar of his rough wool tunic. 'What devil's work is this?' he demanded, clinging to the hope that perhaps Geoffrey, always more vicious than his brother, might be here and not Henry after all. 'Tell me, churl.'

'It is the devil –' the man began to blubber, tears running down his blackened face. 'The devil of Anjou – they are all devils – what matter which one?'

William released him suddenly so that the man stumbled before turning to run from the horror of what had once been his home.

A black frown on his face, William rode on into the centre of the village. The church itself was not burning and it was there by the steps that William saw his old master.

Henry was surrounded by his knights and his mercenaries, all loaded with plunder, silver chalices and gold plate, jewels from the shrine of St Amadour, while the men and women of the village had been driven back, cowed and anguished. Some were struggling with buckets of water to save their homes, the women trying to salvage pathetic remnants from the ruins. Henry was flushed with excitement and by his side the Earl of Chester was gloating over the prizes they had seized, looking without mercy on the terrified priests huddled together by the church door. Sir Bertran de Born was there, a jeweled cross hanging from the pommel of his saddle, and Gilbert de Clare held a sword that was red with blood.

As William rode up they all turned and Henry urged his horse forward to meet him, his voice high-pitched with excitement. 'Welcome, William, welcome!' he cried with no trace of resentment in his voice. 'You have come in a good hour – you see what we have seized? Now I shall be able to pay more *routiers* and we will beat my father – and Richard, damn his soul to hell.'

William looked round the grisly scene, familiar yet with a fearful difference this time. He searched the faces about the Young King's and saw Gilbert's streaked with dirt. Gilbert gave an expressive shrug and William turned back to the Young King. 'I think, my lord, it is your soul that is in danger from this day's work.'

'Dear God,' Bertran said, 'it is all to be as before! You had best have stayed away, Sir William, if you come back only to preach to us.'

William swung round on him in a swift blaze of anger. 'By Christ's Wounds, Sir Bertran, if you do not hold your tongue it is you who will neither preach nor sing nor speak again!' And such was his tone that for once the troubadour was silent.

'William, it was necessary.' Henry was too exhilarated to heed the exchange. 'Look!' he held up a sword encrusted with jewels, but ancient, 'this is Roland's sword! Isn't it a fine prize? Bertran can make a song about this and my father will know that at last I am to be reckoned with.'

'He will indeed,' was William's dry comment. 'You can terrify a few villagers, pillage a shrine –' he bit back the words. If this meeting was not to end in another quarrel he must stomach his revulsion, and already the sight of his lord was reviving all the old love he had for him more strongly than any other emotion. He dismounted and came to Henry's side, taking his hand and setting his lips to it. 'Sire, you see I wear your ring. I came as you bade me.'

Henry leaned down and put his arm about William's shoulders. 'Thank God you did. I need you, William. This time I must win my way or I think I shall go mad.' His eyes glittered oddly, his face too brightly coloured as he looked down, eager, imploring. 'Will you ride with me?'

The words stirred William, reminding him of another day when once before he had asked the same question. William's answer could be no other than the same. He mounted and brought his horse to Henry's side, ignoring the glowering looks of Randulph de Blundevill, but Gilbert reached out a hand, bidding him welcome. As they rode out of the wretched burning place he asked Gilbert in a low voice if Henry was well. 'He does not look himself, and this – this –' he flung out a hand to indicate the burning houses, a dead man sprawled across a doorstep, 'is not his way.'

'Maybe not.' Gilbert edged his horse away from some smoking cinders, 'But needs must be met. And it's only the heat of the fire in his face.'

On the road north again Henry talked of Limoges and how clever he and Geoffrey had been to slip out from under his father's very nose, leaving a garrison to hold that impregnable castle, how he had tried to tempt the old lion into a trap by promising a reconciliation and how nearly he had made him a prisoner.

'Only Richard foiled my plan at the last moment,' he said and boasted, 'The next time I will take my father and then –'

'Is there no love left between you?' William interrupted: He had a swift mental picture of the Old King and the way in which he used to look at his eldest son, the softening of that hard countenance.

'Oh, I mean him no harm,' Henry assured him. 'He is my father and I'll not forget that, but this time I must and will have my rights.'

He could not be blamed for that assertion, William thought, but the grim sorrow of it, that it should come to this between them!

That night they slept at a farmhouse, the men lying in an orchard under the warm June sky, and when the Young King was ready for sleep in a corner of the one room the place boasted, he beckoned to William and took him by both arms. The blue eyes glistened with sudden tears. 'William,' he spoke in a low voice that the others might not hear, 'William, do you forgive me? I was wrong – Margaret told me. And the other things – I was wrong there too.'

Seeing the flushed face, the old smile that could overcome all the vanity, the betrayals, the instability, William clasped him in return.

'My dear lord –' he began and could say no more. But after a moment he realised Henry's hands were unusually hot. 'You are feverish, sire. Do you feel ill?'

Henry laughed and threw himself down on the straw bed. 'I am only intoxicated by what we have done today, that is all. And this silly peasant here has a great fire for a warm evening. Lie beside me, William, and tell me all you have been doing.'

William talked until Henry's eyelids fell, but long after the Young King slept he lay awake, his eyes fixed on Roland's sword, hanging from a hook in the wall. To have taken so precious a thing, robbed a hallowed shrine, seemed to him to be a great sin, and this reunion was clouded by it. He would try to persuade Henry to take that, at least, back to Rocamadour. But when he broached the matter in the morning Henry laughed and said, 'When

I am truly King and Duke I will build a new shrine and lay it there myself, but for the moment I will keep it by my side.'

William said no more. Henry's colour had not faded and there was still that odd glitter in his eyes as they set out on the return journey. By noon he was sitting in the saddle, shaken by tremors that convulsed his body, his hands scarcely able to hold the reins. William, gravely anxious now, rode on one side of him and de Born on the other and when they came to Martel it was clear Henry could go no further. As if by common consent William slipped back into his old place, taking charge as he used to do, and it was he who lifted his master out of the saddle, carrying him into the house of one Stephen, a blacksmith, which seemed to offer the most comfort. William laid him on the only bed in the place and covered him with his own cloak.

Henry was mumbling, burning with fever. Once he looked up and muttered, 'William? I thought – you went to Cologne – are we there?'

'No, my lord, we are at Martel. Try to drink this.'

He drank greedily from the cup set to his lips and then lay back, exhausted. 'Oh God, I've the pains of hell in my guts.'

There was no surgeon to be had but the priest of the place came, saying he had some knowledge of medicine. He bled the sick man after which Henry seemed quieter, and left a potion of herbs to be fed to him. William watched by his side all night while the other slept in snatches. About dawn de Born came, all his impish humour gone.

'I will watch now,' he said in a low voice. 'Get some rest, Sir William,' and when William hesitated, he added, 'I swear I will call you if he stirs.'

In the morning the Young King was worse, in the grip of

dysentery; he asked constantly for water but the herb potion made him sick. The long day passed; the priest bled him again and glancing up at the anxious knights shook his head doubtfully.

William sat on a stool beside him. Was it all to end thus, twenty-seven years of life, all the golden promise of youth, the intense charm, the generosity, lost in pride and bitterness that had turned him into little better than a brigand? In one lucid moment Henry looked up at him and seeing the grief on William's face, his household gathered about his mean bed, he said in a faint surprised voice, 'Am I dying? Jesu, I did not think… William,' his hand came out, burning to the touch, and felt for William's, 'send to my father. Bid him come – I would see him once more –'

'At once, sire. I will send my own squire.' William turned and caught John's eye. A moment later they heard the clatter of hooves.

The smith and his wife, awed by so many great men in their house, brought food but few could eat much, though de Blundevill took a whole capon and devoured it hungrily.

Henry was shivering now and the smith built up the fire.

The knights sat about leaning against the walls, some dozing now and then, watching their lord. William and de Born, for once in harmony, sat either side of the dying man – for that death was near no one doubted now.

It was dawn when John d'Erleigh returned and stood hesitantly in the doorway. William rose and came to him. 'Well? Is the King come?'

'No, sir. He says – he says he fears it is another means to lure him from his army. I told him, indeed I did, and he was unsure, I could see that, for he walked up and down all the while and I think once he wept – but he would not come.' John was trembling with fatigue and misery. 'He only sent this –' and he held out his hand, a heavy gold ring lying in it.

'God have mercy on us all,' William said, and taking the ring went to kneel beside his master. Henry stirred, the tired, red-rimmed eyes opening to focus on William with some difficulty.

'My father – is he here?'

'No, my lord. He would not come – he fears for his safety at our hands.' He saw Henry's face contract and went on hastily, 'But he sends you this ring and with it his love, I am sure of that.'

Tears of weakness were rolling down the Young King's face now. 'Did your squire not say I was dying – did he not know –'

William took one of the hot dry hands in his. 'I know John said all he could but the King would not trust his word – nor ours.'

There was a long silence. Then Henry twisted his head towards the door. 'Bid the priest come then – I must be shriven.' While they waited he lay silent again, only once he turned to William and said in a faint voice, 'God is punishing me – don't you see? And St Amadour. Take the sword back, William – and the rest. I have offended my father too – and you – and so many others, Jesus pardon me …' His voice faded to a whisper.

The priest came and they all withdrew out of earshot. William stood outside with folded arms, his eyes on the blue June sky, swallows wheeling towards the little stream where the mill wheel turned slowly. Some of the townsfolk were gathered, waiting, many praying, whatever evil Henry had done, forgotten.

Gilbert stood beside him and once William spoke, asking where Queen Margaret was.

'In Paris,' Gilbert answered. 'Our lord sent her there when he went to Limoges.'

So there was no hope she could reach her husband before he died. William thought of her grief that must come, for she had loved Henry with all her gentle heart. The thought of her coming widowhood, strangely, made her seem even more remote.

After he had been shriven the dying man seemed calmer and William and the others came in and knelt while the Viaticum was administered, the Host placed on his tongue, his soul prepared for its journey. When it was done he said in a weak but controlled voice, 'Take me from this bed. I am not worthy to die here... lie me on ashes, a rope about my neck – and lay my Cross on me.'

With tears streaming down his face, Sir Bertran de Born helped Gilbert de Clare to do as their master requested, Gilbert cutting a piece of rope and fastening it about Henry's neck, the smith covering a bier with ashes from the forgotten fire, no work done there today.

The priest was intoning prayers as William took from a saddle bag the Young King's Crusader's surcoat, that emblem he had adopted in Limoges Cathedral, red cross on a white ground. This he laid over him and once more Henry reached out for his hand, the feeble fingers scarcely able to clasp it.

'Promise me... promise me, you will take my Cross to the Holy Land ... fulfil my vow? Perhaps then ... God will have mercy –'

William bent and lifted his dying master into his arms. The tears were running down his own face now. He laid one hand on the Cross on Henry's breast. 'I swear it. It shall be done – I swear it in Jesu's name.'

Henry gave a deep sigh. 'I could always – trust you, William. And you have forgiven me –' he paused and then the weak voice trailed on, 'Bear my love to Margaret and ... to my father.' He turned to look at de Born. 'Bertram, don't weep for me ... write me a lament if you will, for one who – gained nothing.'

De Born could not speak for sobbing, his love for the Young King perhaps the only genuine emotion he had ever felt. William held Henry in his arms while the priest prayed and the others answered the words, most of them in tears.

A few moments later Henry moved his head a little against William's chest, the shallow breathing ceased, and it was William who laid him down and folded his hands over the scarlet Cross.

CHAPTER SEVEN

'Do you really want to marry him?' Isabel asked. 'I know he might be king one day if Duke Richard has no heirs, but I would not –'

The Lady Constance glanced at her with superior amusement. 'Child, as if our wants had anything to do with it! Avice will do as the King bids.' She bent to steady her two-year-old son, Arthur, who had stumbled against a stool. 'There – you are not hurt, so don't cry.' She took no notice of his tears and went on, 'When did we women ever have a choice in the matter of husbands? I was betrothed in the cradle.'

'I know.' Isabel bent her head over her embroidery. She was making a stole for the chaplain here at Clare and at each end she was fashioning a dove and a spray of olive leaves to symbolise forgiveness. She was somewhat in awe of Constance who had had two husbands and she wondered now how much she had grieved for Count Geoffrey. The King's third son had been killed two years ago in Paris in a tourney, unhorsed by his opponent. His destrier had trampled on him and he had died of his wounds within a few hours, the grief of the French King Philip such that he had to be restrained from throwing himself upon the coffin. Isabel had met Geoffrey many times and found him delightful company but she had heard that he never kept his word and could be very violent. Little Arthur had been born after Count Geoffrey's death and last year Constance had married again, her new husband Randulph de Blundevill, Earl of Chester.

'I suppose,' Isabel said, 'I would have been betrothed by my father if he had not died when I was so little.'

'I suppose you would,' the Countess agreed, 'though of course it would have been a pity if you had been married to one of those wild Irish lords.' She gave a dramatic shudder.

Avice of Gloucester said, 'I don't see how you can know anything about them as you've never been there. John says –'

'No one should heed what John says about Ireland,' Constance interrupted sharply. 'He caused more trouble there than one would have thought one young man could. For all that Ranulf de Glanville was with him to advise him, even he could not restrain the Prince.'

'He is very young,' Amicia de Clare said in defence of her sister's betrothed. 'Only eighteen now and this was last year.'

'At seventeen Richard was ruling his court in Aquitaine and at the same age Geoffrey was far more of a man,' Constance retorted. She was an attractive woman, though she had never been beautiful, but she had a certain toughness of character that came from her Breton ancestry and she had no time for John's frivolity. 'It is one thing to keep one's subjects under control, quite another to ill-use those he must treat with. I can just imagine him sitting on his throne in Dublin, laughing at the Irish kings who came to do him homage – Jesu, Sir Rama said he even pulled their beards. What a fool! I wonder how Sir Ranulf bore it.'

'John will be King of all Ireland when he goes back,' Avice said in a low voice. There were some things about her betrothed she did not like, but he was handsome and amusing, and she was going to be a loyal wife. 'The Pope has sent him a golden crown made in the shape of peacock's feathers, and if the Pope approves –'

'The Holy Father does not have to subdue all the men John upset,' Constance answered, the mocking note back in her voice. 'Half John's men, and I don't blame them, went over to the natives – what do they call them?'

'Ostmen,' Isabel said, 'at least those who live along the coast. It will be a great thing, Avice, to be married to a King of Ireland whose brother is the future King of England.'

Avice put down her sewing and folded her hands in her lap. She had a natural serenity. 'I think so. At least my lady Constance here has experience enough of marriage to tell us that it is better to have a husband than not to have one.'

Constance pushed her son away from her knees where he was clinging, pulling at the gold fringe of her kirtle. 'Go and play with Gilbert and his sister – there, take your ball.' She watched as he trotted over to where Amicia's children sat on the floor, rolling balls towards a set of skittles. Gilbert said, 'He's too young, lady – he doesn't understand how to play.'

'Then help him,' his mother told him, well aware that her son would rather be out with other boys or waiting in the courtyard for his father's return, but he had a cold in the head and as the wind was in the east she had ordered him to remain within. She wished Avice would not be so tactless and she was glad the Countess was only here for a short visit while her new husband set his affairs in order before accompanying her to Brittany.

Constance leaned back lazily on the cushions of the Lady Amicia's bed, some marchpane between her fingers, and nibbled at the sweetmeat. 'Of course it is better to be wed. I grieved for Geoffrey but I had too great an inheritance for the King not to give me another man. And Randulph is a strong and lusty fellow – he will keep my Bretons to heel.'

Isabel thought of Queen Eleanor whom she attended frequently and who came now sometimes from her less restricted captivity to join the Old King when he held court in England – in fact she had even been allowed to spend Christmas at Chinon a few years ago. Isabel was sure Eleanor had been well able to govern Aquitaine without help from anyone, but Constance was not the woman Eleanor was and anyway she was too indolent. Isabel did not think she herself would have cared for the Earl of Chester as a husband.

She was fifteen now and no doubt when the King came to England, as they said he would soon to raise money for this new crusade that the priests were so ardently preaching, he might remember, busy as he would be, that her marriage was in his gift. Whom would he choose for her? She did not know but she was glad it would not be Prince John. Another face, known so briefly, came before her eyes and brought colour to her cheeks – but she was foolish to think of him. They said he was still unwed, although to her mind he was quite old now – he must be past forty – but she had never met another man who had made so great an impression on her, and although she had been a little girl then she had never forgotten him, nor his kind smile.

And he was coming today, to spend the Christmas season with Gilbert and Amicia. Would he have changed? He had been abroad for five years, ever since the tragic death of the Young King, fighting in Syria. Returning knights and merchants told stories of his heroism, his strength and courage, of the astonishing feats he had accomplished. She listened avidly, but thought so great a man as he must be now would hardly notice her – yet her memories were not of a proud or overbearing man, unless indeed he was greatly changed by all he had done. And he had been her father's friend, perhaps he would want to speak with the King concerning a husband for her, and if he did he would maybe save her from a man of de Blundevill's kind.

Isabel put down her sewing, her chin on her hand. Her hair was plaited and hanging down her back as befitted a virgin but she wore a little white headdress that fastened beneath her small pointed chin, and she hoped she looked well, that this blue gown Amicia had so kindly given her fitted her, shaping a figure now well developed. Her pelisse was edged with marten fur and her white sleeves were long and full, and her shoes she had embroidered herself to match the gown. She was not really vain but she did think blue was the best colour for her to wear for it made her eyes even more vividly blue. She was very fond of her cousin Gilbert and of Amicia and she hoped the King might let her stay here a little longer, certainly while Gilbert's guest was in the house.

It occurred to her that Avice had not answered her question and she bent her head again over her sewing.

'Even if we have no choice in marriage, it is well if we can love our husbands, surely?'

Amicia laughed and nodded, but her sister said, 'It is our duty to learn to love them.'

Avice was more reserved than her eldest sister and she had never forgotten that their grandfather had been Earl Robert of Gloucester, son of King Henry I and brother to the Empress Matilda. Earl Robert might have been a bastard, born of King Henry's mistress in Caen, but he had become a great man and they had royal blood in their veins. Prince John was younger than she was and she could not refute what Constance had said of him, but nevertheless it was a highly prized match. She added a little severely, 'Love is for peasants tumbling in a field,' and Constance laughed, and said. 'Neither of you knows what you are talking about.'

'How should they?' Amicia asked, aware of Isabel's embarrassment. 'I can tell them that respect and affection – aye, and love too – can come after marriage,' and she changed the subject by asking Constance about the kind of embroidery at which the Breton women excelled.

Isabel moved over to the window, away from the fire. It was colder here but she did not mind for she could see down into the courtyard, busy as always, and she could smell roasting meat, the meal being prepared for the return of the Earl of Clare and his guest, and she was still sitting there, half dreaming, when there was a clatter of hooves over the drawbridge and a stream of riders came under the archway.

She knelt upright on the cushioned ledge. There was her cousin Gilbert and beside him a tall man, the hood thrown back from his head, an upright man with long legs. Despite the winter weather his face was tanned, the burnt walnut colour she had seen on other men who had been to

Mediterranean lands – she remembered seeing the Princess Joanna's husband once and his face had been just such a colour – and she longed to see him more closely for she was too far away for smaller details.

After what seemed a long time there was a tap on the door and a page swung it open for the two men to enter, Gilbert to greet his wife first with formal courtesy and then by a swift and passionate embrace, regardless of the other ladies. Then he bowed to the ladies Constance and Isabel before sweeping his son into his arms and fondling his daughter, but Isabel had eyes only for his companion who, in due course, came over to her.

No, he was not changed; he was smiling down at her, his grey eyes warm as she remembered them, the brown hair thick and with scarcely a trace of grey as yet, the moustache covering his upper lip but his chin shaved. She had forgotten how broad his shoulders were, how wide his chest – ah, a woman would be safe with such a man! And then her cheeks were scarlet.

'Mistress Isabel,' he said, 'how pleasant to see you again. But I left a little girl behind.'

It was impossible, despite her nervousness, not to smile back. 'That was some years ago, Sir William. I bid you welcome to Clare. I hope your visit will be a pleasant one.'

He sat down beside her. 'I'm sure it will. I have often wondered for your father's sake where you were, whether you were wed or betrothed.'

'Neither.' Her blush deepened. 'My marriage is in the King's gift, but I stay sometimes with Queen Eleanor – and he – they – he is too busy to consider perhaps –' Aware that she was growing confused, she stopped and then added more calmly, 'Most of the time I spend here with Amicia,'

'And you have been happy?'

'Very.' She gave him a shy smile. 'Amicia is so kind and I love the children. We – we have heard so much about you, messire – so many exciting tales. The troubadours who visit us sing of you.'

'I suppose they must make verses of something,' he said lightly, 'and I have had some good fortune in the Holy Land although,' a graver look crossed his face, 'I went upon so sad a matter.'

'I remember. And I remember the Young King that Christmas at Caen. You must have grieved so much for him and yet…' she paused, wondering whether to go on, and then, surprised at her own daring, did so. 'You were the one to carry out his last wish. That must have comforted you.'

He did not answer for a moment, touched by her perception, surprising in one who had been too young to understand the full wretchedness of that time. Then he said, 'Yes, that is true, Mistress – perhaps that is what kept me there so many years. But since I left matters have not gone well. We had a truce with Sallah-ed-din, which was why I decided the time had come for me to return and I had got to Flanders when I heard that he claimed our knights had broken the truce.' He forgot for the moment that he was talking to a girl, 'There was a bloody battle at Hattin with nearly every Christian man killed or mutilated. Jerusalem has fallen, but you must have heard that. Not one of us can rest now until we have regained the Holy Sepulchre.'

'It is terrible.' She had clasped her hands together, 'We did know – Gilbert's messenger told us. He said the King will ride with the King of France when the time comes.'

'If they can keep peace between them long enough,' William agreed rather sceptically. He knew both men too well. 'Duke Richard plans to sail this spring.'

'Is he to go too? Oh,' a sudden concern showed in her face 'You will go away again so soon?'

'I? No.' He smiled again. 'It takes time to raise men and the money for an army. Duke Richard is nothing if not efficient in these matters and men clamour to go with him for he is a great leader and all know what a fighter he is, but I must offer my services to King Henry. I think he and King Philip do not think to go until next year.'

'You have seen the King since you came back?'

'No.' He paused, looking down at the bustle below, the unloading of pack animals, the men finding room where they might. He could see Jehan and John d'Erleigh arguing with a groom, seemingly about the stabling of his war horses, both burned as brown as he was and John grown into a man. 'No, I have not seen him. I met Gilbert at Ypres and he persuaded me to sail with him to meet our master at Westminster. Now it seems he will not come until the new year after all, so here I am.'

'I am so glad,' she said involuntarily and then lowered her gaze. He seemed for all his friendliness too important now to be interested in her beyond the fact that she was her father's daughter. Later, when he came down to supper wearing a silken surcoat made from a cloth she had never seen, a belt of Moorish design about his waist and a chain of wrought gold hanging from his neck, he seemed a very great man indeed so that she wondered how, while so much in awe of him, she found it so easy to talk with him. That night, in the chamber allotted to him, William lay watching a shaft of moonlight moving slowly across his bed and a similar thought occurred to him. He had never found it easy to talk to a woman other than in polite surface conversation, yet with Isabel it had been different. Perhaps he could once have so confided in Margaret, had he been free to do so; it was his very love for her that had kept him restrained in her presence – but that was a long time ago and now that she was married again, to the King of Hungary, it was unlikely that their paths would ever cross. It was better so – and the old wound, if not forgotten, was healed.

It was strange to be back in England. Riding from the coast he had rediscovered the beauty of the English countryside even in winter – large tracts of forestland full of game, the gentleness of rolling farmland waiting for springtime and seeding, the bare branches of trees making patterns in the road in the pale winter sunlight. A sharp frost under a blue sky exhilarated him, and he wondered how he had endured the heat, the dryness, the flies, of the desert lands for so long. He had had dysentery once, and so had John, but they had both recovered thanks to the attention of a skilled Arab physician and he would be able to advise the King on the care of his troops once they landed at Tyre.

He remembered his last meeting with the Old King, when he had brought him the news of his son's death. Henry had wept and then said simply, 'I trust to God for his salvation.' The Young King had been laid to rest in Rouen Cathedral amidst universal mourning and his father had given William permission to go at once to Palestine to keep his vow. He had set out the next day bearing his dead master's consecrated surcoat, and journeying across Europe had stayed a week with the Princess Joanna, Queen of Sicily. She seemed to him to have all the Plantagenet virtues with none of the vices so prominent in her brothers, and he told her all she wanted to know about them. She grieved for the loss of Henry but it was Richard she wanted to hear of and it was with great reluctance that she bade farewell to William at the end of his stay. Three weeks later he was in Jerusalem.

With awe and reverence he bent low to enter the Holy Sepulchre and there knelt for a long while, reaching out to lay the surcoat with its Cross on the stone slab, to touch the rock where Christ had lain in death, and the thought that He had risen from this very spot filled him with overwhelming wonder. It was something he was never to forget in all his life and he came out into the sunlight again determined to fight the infidel with all his strength, to preserve the places where Christ had walked and taught and died for men.

For a time William had contemplated joining the Knights Templar, that order half monk, half soldier, who gave their lives and their swords to the Christian cause, but in the end the desire to return home proved stronger. He had won a great deal of plunder in his years abroad and brought several laden packhorses with him. He had also acquired another squire, a certain Walter d'Abemon, one of four brothers the eldest of whom, Sir Engerrard, held the manor of Stoke, near Guildford. It had been enfeoffed to the d'Abernons by the first Earl of Clare, and this connection had induced William to take the lad into his service. Walter might not be very quick in the head but he had evinced a dogged devotion for his master and he had a love of horses that further commended him. Furthermore John d'Erleigh had also taken a liking to him and if there was one thing William would not tolerate it was squabbling among his attendants. Despite all this, however, he was still without so much as a manor to call his own, and he was glad to accompany Gilbert to Suffolk.

His mind turned on their arrival. Isabel de Clare had taken him by surprise. As a little girl he had thought her a pleasant enough child and like her father, but now as a woman the resemblance was even more marked. In the few words they had had together she seemed to him to have a quick intelligence, an immediate grasp more of what he left out than of what he did say. He had a sudden swift memory, rising out of the long dead past, of Richard Strongbow's laughing words – 'Maybe I'll give her to you,' and his own reply, 'By that time she will think me a greybeard.'

He had not in all these years thought of marriage, but he thought of it now.

Over the next weeks he spent as much time as he could with Isabel, riding out with her into the frosty woods, the broken twigs cracking beneath their horses' hooves, watching her with one of Gilbert's peregrines on her wrist, sending it off after its quarry, using her lure to bring it back. He commended her on her handling of the bird, though he considered it too strong for her, and when she said eagerly that she did not mind the fierce talons digging into her hand for she loved the sport, he rode to Sudbury one morning to a raiser of falcons. With a keen eye for a good bird as well as a bargain, he bought a little merlin that he thought would sit more gently on her wrist and her delight in it brought him extraordinary pleasure. He watched her too in the hall, playing with the children, listening to the minstrels in the evening, and he contrived to sit beside her at table. Gilbert kept several players to give them music and he danced with her, laughing when she said with daring mischief that she was surprised how well he danced, having supposed that there would be no ladies to dance with in Syria and he might have forgotten how.

'Mark me, wife,' Gilbert said to Amicia within their curtained bed, 'William has his eye on our heiress. Isabel would make him master of Pembroke as well as her Irish lands and Longeuville in Normandy. A great inheritance if King Henry would grant it.'

'Mark me,' Amicia retorted sleepily, 'he is not thinking of that. William is falling in love,' and her husband was too astonished to answer.

William himself was not aware of that, only that he found Isabel delightful company. She was little more than a child and he must seem like an uncle to her but telling himself it was for her father's sake, and because he sensed a certain loneliness beneath her pleasing manner, a loneliness he understood, he found himself seeking her out each time he entered the hall, looking for her before anyone else, being ready to lift her down from the saddle, to walk with her to Mass.

Matters might have gone no further for the moment, but for Gilbert's desire to take his wife with him to visit the Benedictine house at Eye, where his cousin was Prior. William excused himself from accompanying them as he wished to ride to Lavenham to visit a knight he had once fought with in Syria and this seemed a good opportunity.

He was going along the passage to the stair with his mantle over his arm when the Lady Constance, shortly to leave with her son for Brittany, called to him from the bower.

'Are you deserting us too, Sir William?'

He paused in the doorway, and smiled across at Isabel where she sat with Arthur on her knee. 'Only for today, lady. I shall be back tomorrow.'

'And then I have to make this tiresome journey, in midwinter too, to join my lord in Hatfield to ride with him to London. I wish the King had allowed us to wait until the spring.'

'No doubt he feels your country needs its rulers,' William answered formally. He was never at ease with Constance.

She gave him a swift look and then glanced at Isabel, seeing the girl's eyes as she looked across at the knight standing in the doorway. She gave a yawn. 'I think I shall take the Lady Isabel with me. It will make a change for you, child, and perhaps I'll find a fine Breton to husband you.'

Isabel gave a start and her ready colour flooded into her face 'Oh, but – I do not think – my cousin Amicia…'

'Why should she mind? She has her own husband and children to attend to. I'll speak to the King –'

'Madame,' William interrupted with less than his usual courtesy, 'I believe the Lady Isabel is to return to Queen Eleanor shortly, and it is for her grace –'

'The Queen is a prisoner,' Constance said spitefully. She had never liked her mother-in-law and had enjoyed snubbing her in the matter of Arthur's naming, choosing to call him after the man who was a Breton hero instead of after a Norman or Angevin. The Queen had been furious and Constance still relished the memory. 'I think my word will carry some weight with his grace.'

'I doubt it, my lady.'

Constance sat up stiffly, her dark eyes angry. 'You are impertinent, Sir William.'

He laid his cloak on a stool and came further into the room. 'And you, madame, speak discourteously of Queen Eleanor; she is not to be described in those terms. Did you not know she will join the King for Easter at Westminster?'

Constance did not know and she was clearly put out. Then she gave a shrug. 'A show put on for the benefit of the Pope, I imagine – everything must be regular for the sake of this crusade. Anyway, the child's marriage is not in her gift.'

'No,' William agreed. 'It is in King Henry's.'

'True enough, but I –' Constance got up and took her son from Isabel, setting him on his feet. 'I will see that he attends to it soon. It is time and more and she must have a husband –' she paused deliberately, touching Isabel's head with what was meant to be an affectionate gesture, 'a husband who is her equal in rank and possessions.'

For a moment William was too angry to speak and it was Isabel, aware of the veiled insult, who sprang to her feet to answer the Countess.

'My lady,' she said and lifted her head in a manner that reminded William of her father, 'you cannot make me go to Brittany. I wish to stay here with my cousin, or with the Queen.'

'Don't be foolish,' Constance retorted coolly. 'You must not act the child.' She looked the girl up and down. 'You are certainly of an age to be bedded.'

Isabel flushed, her moment of defiance evaporating into awkwardness, aware of William standing so close to her, of his defence of her; and feeling a sudden rush of tears she turned and ran into the inner room.

Constance gave an elaborate sigh. 'Silly child – so emotional. I am sure you will agree, Sir William –'

'Pardon me,' he broke in, 'but I do not think you should discuss this with me. When the Lady Isabel returns to Queen Eleanor no doubt the King will consider the matter.'

'Perhaps.' Constance gave him a sly look. 'And he will consider what a man has in his money chests first, I assure you. But I shall take a hand in it. I hope you have a pleasant journey to your friend – he lives in some small manor near Lavenham, I believe? I think it is going to snow.' She turned away to her embroidery frame and William, bowing stiffly, turned and left her.

He rode away from the castle, his anger fed by the

memory of Isabel in tears, running from the room. By God, it was he who would speak to the King, to Queen Eleanor if he had the chance before that spiteful bitch could take Isabel away – and she so gentle yet with something of the spirit of Richard Strongbow.

He spent the night at his friend's 'small manor', but though he enjoyed the meeting, his mind was on the scene with Constance and he wondered why she had chosen to speak thus to him. Was it because she had some desire to secure Isabel's fortune for one of her own Breton favourites? It seemed likely but quite why she thought him a threat, to the extent of reminding him of his position, he did not know.

In the morning he left earlier than he had intended, anxious to return to Clare. There he found his squires John d'Erleigh and Walter d'Abemon grooming his other horses, for he had only taken Jehan with him. As he dismounted, shaking the light dusting of snow from his mantle, he asked if the Lady Constance had gone.

'Aye, sir,' John told him. 'She left over an hour ago.' He added, a faint smile on his face, 'I fear she did not like the inclement weather – her squires and ladies will not have a pleasant journey.'

Thank God she has gone, William thought, and strode off into the hall and up the stair, intending to seek Isabel, half hoping she might be alone in the bower. But there, at the top of the spiral, he saw her. She was sitting on a stone ledge by a window, staring out across the moat to the flat meadows and the leafless trees beyond.

'Child,' he said, 'what are you doing here? It is cold and there must be a fire in the bower.'

She raised her head and he saw a sadness in her face that was oddly touching. 'It is – a little cold, but there is so much chatter in the bower, and – and I wanted to be quiet.'

He took her hand and found it icy, and throwing off his cloak wrapped it about her shoulders. Then he sat down beside her, 'At least the Countess has gone,' he said. 'I am sorry she spoke as she did yesterday, but pay no heed to her: King Henry is not likely to do so where your marriage is concerned.'

She twisted her head away. 'I do not think I want to be married.'

'What else is there?' he asked, half smiling, 'unless –' and the smile went, 'unless you wish to enter a convent?'

'Oh no,' she answered swiftly. There was a little pause and then she gave a deep sigh. 'I know I must wed at the King's command, that it must be for state reasons or for land or because he wishes for some alliance, but I wish it could be to someone who – who –'

'Yes?' Involuntarily he had taken her cold hands and was warming them between his own, lifting them to hold close to his breast. 'A man who could care for you, love you, Isabel?' And then he knew why he had been so angry yesterday. He put both hands, so small in his brown ones, to his lips. 'But Constance was right in one thing. I have nothing, no land, no standing. I am a knight and no more.'

'But I have enough for two –' she began impulsively and then stopped, her face suffused.

He gave a low laugh, glanced up and down the passage to be sure it was empty, and then letting her hands go, put both arms about her to draw her into their circle. 'Isabel! Is it possible? Would you take me, landless fellow that I am?'

'Oh yes, yes,' she whispered, her face against the warm blue wool of his pelisse. 'If I thought that you –'

'I love you,' he said and astonished himself, 'and I have never wanted to wed before.'

She kept her face hidden. 'And I you – oh, I think from that first moment I saw you, six years ago. Only I did not think you would notice me.'

'It is the other way about. You are an heiress and I am no match for you, as the Countess rightly hinted, though why she should have thought it necessary, I don't know. Perhaps she saw more than we guessed.'

'She is a horrid woman,' Isabel retorted in a muffled voice, and a note of fear crept into it. 'But she is the Countess of Brittany and the King's daughter-in-law. Maybe he will listen to her and make me wed some fierce Breton. I have heard terrible tales of those people.'

'You shall not marry where you don't wish,' he said, so sharply that she started and looking up saw his face set in determination. 'It is I who shall speak to the King,' he went on, 'but are you sure? I am forty-two, Isabel, and you are fifteen. It would be more fitting if you were to wed a younger man.'

'Oh no.' She shook her head with equal determination. 'I do not want to marry anyone else. I never have.'

He looked down at her in surprise and then, as he read her face, he was aware of happiness, of a joy he had never known. The corridor was still empty and holding her closer he bent his head and kissed her and nothing that had gone before seemed to matter.

At last he raised his head and she settled hers against his shoulder with a contented sigh, but after a moment he said, 'Isabel, we must consider – the King may well tell me I am presuming too far to ask for you. Quite apart from the fact that he may have some baron in mind for you, a far better marriage, I was in rebellion against him before I went to Syria, and although in a sense he pardoned me for the sake of his son, he may not look kindly on me when I make such a request of him.'

'He will; he must be glad and grateful for what you did for the Young King. Besides,' she added fiercely, 'I will tell him I will take no other man. If I have to I will take only the veil, for I won't wed anyone but you. I am not Richard Strongbow's daughter for nothing.'

He gave a low amused laugh. 'By Our Lady, you are not. I've never told anyone this, but once when you were six months old your father said, only he was half joking, that when you were grown he might give you to me.'

'Did he? Oh!' Suddenly bold, she sat upright and catching one of his hands held it to her cheek. She had always been in such awe of him but now, now that he had confessed his love, they had come together somehow on the same level, and her father's approval set the seal on it. 'Then I am determined. I will marry you, Sir William or,' a little smile lifted her mouth, 'or I will enter the nunnery near here and become Prioress and be very horrid to all my nuns because I could not have the man I wanted.'

After that he could only put his lips to hers again, their laughter merging into more kisses.

But it was not going to be easy, he knew that. He was the second son of a minor landowner and his elder brother John had a son to succeed to their small property; he had fame, enhanced perhaps by all he had done in Syria, but he did not know how the Old King would view him now.

He spoke to Gilbert who raised his eyebrows and said cryptically, 'Amicia is wiser than I, it seems. Well, William, I wish you well. I would welcome your alliance with my family, you know that, and Isabel would make you a good wife, I think, apart from the possessions she would bring you. Amicia says she sews well and has a considerable knowledge of herbs.' He belched and slapped his stomach. 'She made a brew that eased the gripes in my bowels, I can tell you.'

William was shaken with laughter. It was good to have the approval of Gilbert and Amicia, and he thought in later years he would remember the days of his courtship as days of laughter.

CHAPTER EIGHT

At Easter the King wore his crown at Westminster and Queen Eleanor sat beside him. William and Gilbert rode in with the Countess Amicia and the Lady Isabel, and at the first opportunity William sought out his friend Will. Will FitzHenry had gained renown himself, grown so tall and with such long arms that he had been nicknamed Longsword and was considered a great man at the jousting. He and his chancellor brother accompanied the King everywhere these days and as he and William stood talking together in the hall, cups of ale in their hands, William told him frankly what he wanted.

'You aim high,' Will said, 'but not too high, by God. You have earned all that and more.'

'But will the King think so? He may remember – other things.'

Will shrugged. 'He is unpredictable, as always, but I'll wager my new percheron that he receives you favourably. He always admires brave deeds and we have heard a great deal about your doings. Apart from that – but I'll say no more,' Will finished. 'I'll go to him now on your behalf.'

'Say only that I want to pay homage to him after so long away. Let me see if the moment is right for the other matter.'

It was before supper that same evening that William was summoned to the King's chamber and he was surprised at the speed with which his request for an interview had been granted. He found the King in his bedchamber, alone except for Geoffrey the chancellor and his body servant. He was wearing only shirt and hose and about to have a fine gown of purple velvet flung over his head. At a motion from his hand, the servant paused and William knelt.

'Well, Sir William,' Henry looked down at him, 'so you are returned to us. There's scarce been a week we've not had some knight or chapman telling us tales of you. Is it true that you once dispatched twelve Saracens single-handed when they ambushed you?'

'Fourteen, your grace.' William saw no point in being modest about a matter that still afforded him grim satisfaction. 'But I did have my squire with me and they were not Sallah-ed-din's best men.'

Henry laughed and motioned to his servant to finish dressing him while he questioned William keenly about Syria, about the climate, the requirements of troops who were to fight there, talking of his own proposed expedition with the French King. 'Half my age, of course,' he said crisply, 'but by Jesu, there's fight enough left in me yet and experience can teach the young a few tricks, eh? Now tell me,' he went on in his usual brisk manner, asking penetrating questions until he remembered he had not yet bidden William to rise. He said abruptly. 'Why have you come to me? I need not ask if you carried out your commission?'

'No, your grace.' William told him of the Holy Sepulchre, the stone tomb, and his son's Cross lying briefly upon it, the prayers offered for his soul.

Henry's business-like manner had faded, an intense weariness creeping over him, 'He made a better business of dying than living. Two sons I have lost and both died at enmity with me – even Richard will turn against me again if it suits him. Bastards, all of them.' He flung an arm impulsively round Geoffrey's shoulders. 'Here are my true sons, he and his brother.'

'And John, your grace?' William asked the question cautiously.

'Ah, John –' a softer expression crossed the King's face. 'John is young and makes mistakes but he is loyal to me. He loves me as none of the others did, though God knows I loved Henry as I have loved no one else on this earth. He cost me much suffering, he emptied my money chests, but I would he had lived to cost me more. You loved him too,' he paused, his eyes fixed sombrely on William, 'and for that I forgive you much. I forgive Bertran de Born for the same reason. He wrote a lament for Henry – *no man rejoices in these bitter days ... now he is fallen to the great lord Death* – and bitter days they were.' He seemed to brace himself. 'But past, William, and I am glad to see you again. What do you want of me?'

'To renew my homage to you, sire.' William held up his hands, palms together, but for a moment he knew swift fear. Henry would pardon him, he was sure of that now, but what if he should refuse the further request. What reason had he indeed to grant it? He thought of Isabel, waiting in the bower with the Queen, as nervous as he was. All his hope of her lay in the will, the whim perhaps of this man here, unpredictable as Will Longsword said, but just and sometimes generous.

The short strong hands were set about his. 'Come back into my service then, William Marshal, and into my household. I have a place about me for a man such as you, and for what you did for my son, for journeying so far to obey his dying wish, I would give you some recompense.' He raised William to his feet. 'You have no lands of your own; is that perhaps something you wish for?'

'I would have land, yes, your grace, but there is something more than that, though land is concerned.' As always, William thought, Henry would appreciate plain speaking, and he went on, 'I would ask a greater gift, one you may not wish to bestow on me.'

The King raised his sandy brows. 'Oh? What is it you want that is so serious a matter?'

'The Lady Isabel de Clare for my wife.'

He had taken Henry entirely by surprise. The King sat down on the edge of the bed and glanced at his bastard son who was equally astonished, Will not having confided in him. Henry set his elbows on his knees and surveyed William, his eyes narrowing. 'You would be Earl of Pembroke, lord of Leinster, as well of Longueville in Normandy? You ask a great deal, William, and the girl is little more than a child.'

'Fifteen, sire, of marriageable age – and I would ask for her if she had no dowry at all.'

Henry stared at him and for a moment William saw the whole business hang in the balance. Mother of God, he prayed, let me have her!

Then the King burst into a great guffaw. 'William, you have been snared by a pretty face! Jesu, I thought you'd end your days a bachelor. And she –'

'I think she will not be unwilling,' William put in hastily and the King looked even more surprised.

'I was not considering that; the girl will do as I bid her. I was merely thinking I might have got her a younger, richer husband –'

'I know I have little to offer.' William was aware that his voice sounded stiff, that what pride was in him resented the words he had to speak.

'– but not a better man,' Henry finished as if William had

not interrupted. 'You shall have the girl. You have earned your earldom and if your marriage bed brings you love as well, I'm glad of it. Most of us find there are a few thorns in it as well.' He saw the swift light in the face opposite him. 'Well, well, go and find her and tell her what I have said. I will set the clerks to drawing up the documents,' and as he waved William to the door he added in a low voice, 'I pray God you will have more joy in your sons than I have had in mine.'

The preparations for the Crusade went ahead. Henry held a great council at Geddington in Northamptonshire where the Archbishop of Canterbury preached a fiery sermon exhorting all men to join the King in his holy war. The Jews were forced to contribute handsomely, and taxes were levied up and down the country. There was much grumbling and Will Longsword said, 'What a lot of grasping fellows they must be who could deny their fat purses for Our Lord's cause.' To which William replied that it was not only the fat purses that were being emptied, every man down to the meanest serf was taxed to the limit.

They were both to go with the King and for William the prospect of the coming journey was tempered with a certain reservation. The King was too busy to hurry forward the necessary settlement and when William broached the subject of his marriage all he got was a broad smile, a crude joke and an injunction to exercise patience.

But Isabel was to be his, that was all that mattered, though it seemed hard at his age to be faced with the prospect of having to wait at least two, maybe more, years for her. For God knew how long this great army assembling on both sides of the channel would take to journey to Palestine, drive out the infidel and journey home again, and it was with a graver face than usual that he set about his own preparations, buying new gear, setting up his squires John and Walter. The thought that on his marriage day he would receive an earldom and other lordships was of less importance, though he could not but be gratified that at last he would stand on equal footing with such men as Geoffrey of Mandeville and Randulph de Blundevill.

Hubert Walter, the clerk who had brought John d'Erleigh to him, was now Dean of York and in his cool way seemed pleased, wishing William well and promising him his prayers. A cold, competent fellow, William thought, but one who would be a loyal friend, and he had a liking for the man's honesty.

And then all the plans, the preparations, were cast into the shadow by news from France. William was summoned to the King's great chamber in the palace of Westminster to find Henry pacing furiously. Will was there and the chancellor and Gilbert de Clare and several other barons, all as precipitously ordered into the King's presence.

He had a letter in his hand and his face was mottled with rage. 'By God's Wounds!' he swore. 'Is nothing to be honoured, no trust sacred? You there –' he threw the letter to a clerk, 'read it to us again, that we may all hear it.'

The clerk read carefully, meticulously, his very slowness adding to the King's impatience. It seemed that the old quarrel had broken out again between Duke Richard and the Count of Toulouse over a matter of some Poitevin merchants that the Count had seized. He had them blinded and castrated, apparently in revenge for some incursion of Richard's, and the Duke, furious, promptly invaded Toulouse with no reference to its overlord, the French King. Philip at once broke the truce agreed upon when they had all taken the Cross, and he marched south, seizing Angevin castles as he went, burning crops, slaying

King Henry's subjects, while he sent a second army storming into Normandy.

The clerk laid the letter down with a shaking hand and retreated behind his table. His royal master's face was purple with tiny suffused veins, his eyes bulging. He had a pair of gloves in his hand and he stuffed one into his mouth, tearing at the fingers with his teeth in a paroxysm of rage. Then as the gathered barons exchanged glances, he flung the gloves down and with one gesture swept letter, pens and inks from the table to fall into a heap on the floor, the ink running over the scattered parchments

'God hear me!' he bellowed. 'I will tame them both! Richard and Philip shall learn who is the man still! Whelps both of them to be beaten, by God! We leave at once.'

'Sire,' the Earl of Clare began tentatively. 'It is five o'clock, near the supper hour.' Gilbert did not relish the thought of a snatched piece of fowl eaten on horseback. 'Surely in the morning –'

Henry showed his teeth. 'Fill your belly if you must, but a summer evening's light will get me far on my way and the laggards must catch me up.'

William and Isabel had only a few moments in which to say farewell. She was crushed in his arms, trying not to cry, her happiness at their betrothal lost in this present misery.

'I will come back,' he said, one hand stroking her hair: 'Beloved, I will return, I promise you.'

'You cannot say that.' She raised her head to look up at him. 'You will fight the French King and Duke Richard and then you will go with King Henry to the Holy Land and I will not see you for years – if you come back at all. I can't bear it – I can't bear it.'

'Dear love,' he said, 'I have been fighting since I was a

boy with barely a scratch on me to show for it. I know how to care for myself. Only trust me and if we have to wait, pray that it may not be for too long.' But over her head he gave a little sigh. It might be hard to be patient at fifteen but it was even harder when one felt the years slipping away, the lost and empty years, before he might have her for his own. Nor, despite his words, did he delude himself that men did not die in battle, or in that hot disease-ridden land where fever and dysentery were as much enemies to the men of the west as Sallah-ed-din and his heathen hordes.

She flung up her arms about his neck, reaching up to him: 'If we were only wed now, if I could only come with you –'

There was no answer to that. Queen Eleanor would care for her, he knew that, but this parting was tearing from him the heart he had not known until so recently that he possessed. He bent his head, his mouth on hers, twisting the fair plaits in his hands, her small body pressed against his.

A moment later he was walking away from her and he did not turn to look back.

King Henry was ill, had been ill for months with a disease the doctors seemed unable to cure. He groaned with pain, clasping his hands over his belly; sometimes he vomited and the dark colour of it caused his doctors to shake their heads. He was lying on his bed, sweating and restless, in the castle of Saumur in the early days of the January after he had left England, when William Marshal and Bertrand de Verdun came to him.

'Well?' he asked in a weak voice utterly unlike his normal tones. 'What did my son have to say?'

'My lord.' William came to the bed. 'We could not overtake Duke Richard. We learned at Amboise that he has issued letters summoning all his men to his standard. He means war.'

The King groaned out loud. 'God, why am I so punished?' He paused and looked from one to the other. 'Why does my son love the French King more than his own father? Tell me – '

Bertrand de Verdun, a man of few words, glanced at his companion and motioned to him to tell the tale. Verdun had experienced Plantagenet rage before and though this man was sick there was no saying what he would do when the devil was roused in him.

'Sire,' William began, 'he has ever gone his own way, you know that. And this time –' he broke off. What was there to say, what crumb of comfort for an ageing, deserted father? He thought of all that Henry had achieved: the stable government in England, wise laws administered on the whole justly by well chosen public servants, a rule that was hard but fair; whereas Richard, though he was a disciplinarian, sought his own military glory and his own independence first. Yet in a sense William understood the frustration that drove the Duke to distraction.

It was a difficult situation they had returned to last June. Henry's armies held the French at bay in Normandy and at length in the autumn a conference was called, mainly because the Counts of Blois and Flanders refused to aid King Philip while he broke the truce agreed on for the period of the Crusade. Richard, ostensibly joining his father, suddenly submitted the matter of Toulouse to the French King without reference to his father, who was justifiably angry. The Duke demanded yet again the hand of Princess Alice and again Henry temporized. Richard made an ugly innuendo, Philip turned the argument to his own account, and Richard in a blatant about-face did homage to him for his lands. Faced by such treachery, Henry agreed to a further truce and was stunned to see his son leave arm-in-arm with Philip. It was then that he sent Marshal and de Verdun to see what Richard meant by his desertion. And they had returned with no answer to that question.

A miserable Christmas feast passed at Saumur. Henry recovered a little but was in a bad temper and glowered throughout. Even Princess Alice, still in her place beside him, could not take the gloom from his face. William ate in silence and thought of Isabel.

'God save us,' Gilbert de Clare said, 'I'm fond enough of the wench but who would have thought William would lose his head over her?'

'You will lose his friendship if you say that to him,' Will Longsword told him and Gilbert was somewhat relieved when a few days later the King sent him on a mission to England.

Prince John made some pretence of enjoying the twelve days of feasting but there was a crafty look in his face that made William suspicious, and he wondered why the Prince's knights appeared to be in a constant state of alertness. He was hardly surprised therefore when John requested permission to visit his Norman castles. The King granted it and John rode away northwards. Soon after there were other conspicuously empty seats as other lords found reason to visit their domains.

Spring came with the failure of all negotiations. French troops broke the Norman borders and swept down into Maine. Henry was at Le Mans, his own town, his birthplace. To the west the Bretons had joined Richard who was menacing him from the south and, hemmed in on all sides, in grim danger, with a mere six or seven hundred knights left to him, the old Lion roused himself once more.

A dusty man-at-arms rode in to say that the French army was advancing but he knew nothing of the numbers. Henry, busy about the fortifications, sent William out to reconnoitre. William left the castle without his heavy mail and wearing only a sword at his side; he took John with him and two other knights only. It was early on the morning of Sunday the eleventh of June and as they slipped out of the town William could only think of the Young King who had died in his arms on this day six years ago. Soon the bells would be ringing for Mass and in every church prayers would be offered for the soul of the King's dead son.

At the gates the four of them dismounted and went out on foot, William leading the way northwards along the bank of the river Huisne. The mist was thick, the sun not yet breaking through, and for a while there was silence, the water sluggish, only the occasional scuffle of a water rat or the sound of a duck quacking lazily broke the stillness. None of them spoke and as they went William wondered what the Young King would have done in the face of this present conflict. Looking back now from a distance he realised with sorrow and some cynicism that the younger Henry could not have been relied on to jump either way. Urged on by unscrupulous tale-bearers, the Plantagenet brood had come to believe they were descended from the Devil and could behave as sons of evil. William crossed himself, offered up a brief prayer for his dead master's soul and concentrated on the business in hand.

There were other sounds now, all too familiar – the heavy rhythm of hooves approaching, the thud of marching feet, the jingle of accoutrements. 'Keep down,' William hissed and they flattened themselves behind the bank, peering out through some alder bushes.

The whole of the French army was passing along the road on the further side, a vast army. At the forefront rode King Philip himself – though King Philip did not like war and preferred the Council chamber or the tree at Gisors for settling his problems – and beside him was the tall, martial and magnificent figure of Duke Richard.

The pennons and standards hung limply as they passed, but the mist was beginning to lift, a pale circle of sun trying to penetrate, with all the promise of a bright June day to come. William slithered backwards down the bank and beckoned to his companions.

Henry was coming from Mass when they returned, his face grey, his eyes showing the depth of his sorrowful memories, but he became alert on the instant. He ordered the bridge to be broken down, the ford blocked, all the banks strengthened. But the next day, riding out with William and a few followers, he saw the French sounding for another ford. It seemed they had had some local help for a sudden yell of triumph carried across the water and a party of Frenchmen plunged in, splashing through the shallows.

The King and his small contingent hastily retreated towards the gate. 'Go in, sire, go in!' William shouted. 'I'll hold them. For God's sake, get him in, Will!' A dozen knights ranged themselves beside him, including the young Earl of Essex, Geoffrey de Mandeville, who was burning to distinguish himself, while Will Longsword and the rest hurried the King through the gates.

The French caught up with the rearguard in the jumble of houses outside the walls and there was fierce hand-to-hand fighting. William struck out at an exultant face, saw the blood as he split the skull and the man went down under plunging hooves. He dealt more blows, warded off a mace swung high at him and caught sight of young

Essex bearing himself well. They held the enemy, keeping the road clear, though William was grimly aware that if reinforcements came up they would be hopelessly outnumbered, but as yet he dared not withdraw his little force nor leave the enemy free in the suburbs.

The end came suddenly. Some Frenchmen, seeking to clear the way to the gate, set fire to a few houses; a breeze had got up and was fanning the flames towards the whole of the town so that in a short time the fire was out of hand. The French slipped away, their work done for them, but not before William had slain two more knights and de Mandeville driven his sword into another's guts. The Frenchmen fell into the mess of blood and cinders in the road and William ordered his men through the gates. These closed behind him, the great bars were set into place, and he rode up to the castle where, hot, grimy and blood-stained, he sought the King.

Henry was in consultation with his chief men. 'We must retreat,' he was saying savagely. 'God's curse on them! William, what do you say? Is the fire spreading?'

'It is, my lord, the wind is against us. I think you should leave before the French attack in force. We shall only be burned if we stay here.'

'Then we go,' Henry said, 'towards Fresnay – at once, by the south postern.'

Fifteen minutes later, with his pitifully small force he turned his back on Le Mans, his birthplace. The flames were consuming the town and he gave a harsh and bitter laugh. 'Do you know, William, my grandfather the Conqueror received his death wound in that city? I think it is my death wound too.'

'I pray God not, sire.'

'Pray?' Henry's face was convulsed and he looked up into the sky. 'God does not hear prayer. He has taken everything from me, my sons, my honour, this place, and I – I –' He ground his teeth in fury, glaring up at the blueness above. 'I will make recompense to You, jealous God! Not one prayer will I offer again, not one!'

'My lord!' William was shaken by the biting despair, shocked by such blasphemy. 'My lord, your fortunes will turn. God has not deserted us.'

'You think not?' Henry turned and William with him to look back at the burning place, the hill on which it stood a mass of flame. As they did so they saw a troop of the enemy tearing at full gallop out of the west gate, swerving towards the road they had taken.

William snatched up his reins. 'I'll hold them,' he said once more. 'Go, your grace – I need only a few men. Get you to Fresnay and I'll follow.'

The King flung out a hand and seized his. 'By God, I never had so loyal a man,' and Will cried out, 'God be with you, Marshal.'

William turned back, taking the last twenty men with him, refusing de Mandeville and ordering him to stay with their lord. Then he set his face back towards Le Mans with his little troop, cutting off through a copse to surprise the enemy. The leader of the French was outstripping his own men in his eagerness and it was as he came headlong down the road that William saw that the figure was familiar, that in his determination to seize his father, believing his victory absolute, Duke Richard had for once allowed his feelings to get the better of his judgement.

William dug in his spurs and brought his horse out from among the trees, drawing it up sharply on its haunches not twenty yards from Richard. He had his lance in his hand and for the first time saw fear in the Duke's face.

'Don't slay me!' Richard cried out and tugged at the reins. 'Can't you see? I've come after my father, unarmed. We've won the day and it's enough – it's enough. God's mercy, Marshal, hold your hand!'

William gave him a grim, hard smile. 'I never thought to see this. I shall not kill you, Duke Richard' – over the Duke's shoulder he could see his followers coming up fast, and he added, – 'I will leave that to the Devil.' He drew back his arm and threw his lance with expert aim so that it plunged deep into the neck of Richard's horse. The animal fell, his rider with him. And such was the confusion among the Duke's followers as they came up that William and his men escaped without hindrance to join the King.

Two days later they were at Chinon and could breathe safely. 'Holy Saints,' Will said, 'I did not think we would come alive out of that – nor see you again, William.'

'I'll die in my bed yet,' William retorted.

But the situation was little better. Philip's host was too great and a good many Norman barons were reluctant, even on Henry's orders, to attack their suzerain – and Henry himself was ill again. The old sickness had recurred and in the scrap by the gate he had been slightly wounded in the heel; little more than a scratch but it was turning septic and every day grew more painful, lines of red inflammation creeping up his leg.

Princess Alice came to Henry's chamber with a physician, tending the King herself, sponging his face with a damp cloth, holding his head while he sipped a cooling drink. She was thirty-two now, still betrothed to Richard, still at Henry's side, and she asked the physician in a fierce voice if he would live. The man looked doubtful and her eyes met William's across the bed. He could read what thoughts were in her mind: if the King died what then would she do, what would Richard, her brother Philip, demand of her? William said nothing. In all justice, he thought, she had brought this situation on herself and he had never liked her. But then in the old days his eyes had been all for Margaret and Alice's invidious position meant nothing to him. He left her to the nursing and sat in the hall with Will and de Mandeville, a heaviness lying on them as they waited.

The Count of Flanders, a sensible and politic man, came to Chinon and suggested that the King should make terms with Philip and Duke Richard. Henry called his bastard sons to him and wished that John were not so far away, holding for him in Normandy. William and de Mandeville also came to his chamber with Walter of Coutances, Archbishop of Rouen, and he asked their advice.

'Treat, my lord,' the Archbishop begged. 'You are ill, you cannot go on.'

No one could disagree with this and wearily the King nodded, but he added, 'All I need is rest. I'll get my strength back and then by God, Richard had best look to himself.'

Four days later William sat on a stool by a narrow window and looked out into the darkness. There was a moon but it was hidden behind heavy thunder clouds rolling in from the west. Duke Richard had no more need to fear his father's vengeance, for the man lying on the bed was clearly dying. They had been four wretched days, days of humiliation and despair, of pain and defeat. The King and his inner council had gone to Colombières, the place appointed for the meeting, and on the way had spent the night at a Commandery of the Knights Templars, where he had been so ill that it was feared he could not go on. William had talked for a long time with Amaury, the Master of the Commandery whom he had known for many years, remembering how once he had thought of joining the Templars – but that was before he had loved

Isabel.

The King insisted on going on in the morning and at Colombières Philip showed concern for the sick man. He saw that his old enemy was not fit to sit in the saddle and offered to have a cloak laid for him on the ground. Duke Richard said sternly that if his father thought illness was a way to treat for better terms he was mistaken.

Jesu, William thought, is there no trust left anywhere? They must see this was no sham and when Henry refused to dismount, he and Chancellor Geoffrey sat their horses on either side of the King, ready to support him if he fell. But he had stuck grimly in the saddle, clinging to the pommel and agreeing one by one to the ignominious terms – to do homage to Philip, to surrender Princess Alice, to make his barons swear fealty to Richard, to surrender a number of castles, to keep his vow to go on the Crusade.

Watching the scudding clouds William felt his anger rise again at the memory of that last demand. He could see Philip and Richard, both young men – Richard thirty and the French King less – relishing it, aware of the mockery of it, that they used that ultimate weapon of youth to bludgeon a sick old man. Henry was forced to give his son the kiss of peace and William had heard him mutter, 'I'll not die until I've had my revenge on you – traitor!'

Only one concession he had gained, that a list of the allies on both sides should be made, and he sent his seal keeper, Roger Malchet, to see it done.

The King groaned suddenly and stirred. The physician had gone to his own bed for there was nothing more he could do, and it was William and Geoffrey who watched beside him. Geoffrey was nodding against the wall and William rose softly and came to the King. He bathed the flushed and swollen face, straightened the bedclothes.

The King's eyes opened and out of a fog of memory he muttered, 'William? Was it hot in Jerusalem? I am so hot. You took his Cross – you were his friend –' he broke off, mumbling unintelligibly. Then he said quite clearly, 'I have held so much – but God is angry. I – I blasphemed Him, did I not?'

Geoffrey had woken now and come to the other side of the bed. 'His mercy is greater than His anger, my lord. I will pray, we will all pray.'

Henry's eyes rested on him. 'You have been the best of sons, you and Will. Call Will, I would see him.'

William rose silently and sent a sleepy page for Will, and the three of them knelt by the bed. The King was quieter now. For a while he lay and listened to the ominous roll of thunder, and a flash of lightning illuminated the drawn face. 'A storm is coming,' he said, 'but I think my storms are over. William,' he reached out a hand and William took it, 'whatever is to be done I can trust you and these my sons to do it. I leave all in your hands.'

Daylight came and the storm died. The King was shriven and some semblance of peace came into the wan features. In the afternoon Roger Malchet returned and with him a shattering of that peace. At the King's command he read the list of names and at the end came to a sudden halt.

'Well?' the King asked weakly. 'Is that all?'

'No – no, sire,' Malchet answered in a low voice. 'There is one other, but I dare not –'

'By Christ and His Cross!' Henry roused himself once more, struggling to his elbow. 'You will speak, Malchet, or feel a rope about your neck. Tell me –'

Malchet retreated slightly, but he said, 'The last name, my lord, the last name – is that of – Prince John.'

Henry cried out and fell back on the pillow. 'Not John? Not my John? Everything I have done has been for him.'

He gazed at Malchet, saw nothing but the truth in the seal-keeper's frightened face, and turned his own into the pillow. 'Then there is nothing left to live for.' In a broken voice words tumbled from him. 'Shame – shame on a conquered King – shame that his own flesh should betray him.'

Geoffrey, his plump face disfigured by tears, lifted his father into his arms that the lion might lie more comfortably, resting against him. The King spoke no more. The three watchers remained where they were in silence and about noon the laboured breathing ceased.

The King was carried to Fontevrault, his bier set beneath the soaring vaults and ribbed columns of the abbey he had favoured above all others. In the light of tall funeral candles the nuns watched, praying for his torn and restless spirit.

'*Requiem aeternam dona eis, domine, et lux perpetua luceat eis…*' their voices reiterated, and William, kneeling in the dark shadow of a pillar, echoed the words.

The day's events at Chinon had been horrifying. He had gone with Will and Geoffrey to see messengers sent with the tidings to Duke Richard, the heir, and to King Philip – would Philip rejoice at the death of his enemy? – to England to Queen Eleanor and to Prince John in Normandy. And on their return to the death chamber they found the servants gone with everything they could lay their hands on. Knowing how low the King's resources had become they had taken what they could in recompense for their services. It was William who had covered the King's body, found suitable raiment and jewels for the burial.

Now he knelt, praying for Henry's soul and thinking at the same time of the change in fortune that it might mean to him. Henry had promised him Isabel, but would

Richard honour that promise? Would Richard want to see him Earl of Pembroke, Lord of Leinster, Sieur of Longueville? If not what should he do? He thought of her, ignorant as yet of what had happened, waiting for him, and he could have groaned aloud. He would have her somehow, despite Richard, despite every obstacle, yet he knew he could not storm into Winchester castle and abduct her – what life could she have with a man who thus outlawed himself? Mother of God, he prayed, help us, for Jesu's sake.

He was deep in his thoughts, his eyes on the tall yellow candles, the bier, the circle of kneeling black figures surrounding a face at peace at last – perhaps God had forgiven that blasphemy on the road from Le Mans – when there was a creak as the small south door opened.

It was Richard, clad in a black cloak and alone. He strode across the stone flags to stand in silence, looking down at the face of his father. After a moment he knelt, crossed himself, and then rising left as silently and impassively as he had come.

CHAPTER NINE

King Richard rode to Chinon to claim his own and in the great circular hall William Marshal waited with the half-brothers of the new King and the few members left of the previous royal household.

'I fear for you,' Will said in a low voice as they heard the hooves of a vast mesnie clatter into the courtyard. 'My brother will remember that encounter outside Le Mans.'

'Aye,' Geoffrey added, 'you bested him, William, and he was never one to like that. And how he will view us, only

God knows.'

'I regret nothing I have done,' William said. He was richly dressed this morning in his eastern silk mantle, wearing his gold chain and elaborate sword belt. If he was going to be dismissed he would at least go out with dignity. 'I trust in God, who has ever helped me since I became a knight.' But he knew it was a moment of decision that might mean a reversal of all he had achieved.

Richard came in attended by his brother John and a large company of barons and knights, fully caparisoned in mail and helm and as imposing as ever. He paused at the door and without taking his eyes off the three awaiting him, removed his helm, handing it to a page who sprang alertly to receive it. His face was expressionless as they came forward to kneel before him. He looked slowly from one to the other. 'I am your King,' he said at last. 'Well, Geoffrey?'

His half-brother raised both hands. 'Your man, sire, life and living,' and Richard covered them, repeating the gesture as Will raised his.

Then he turned to their companion. 'And you, William Marshal? What have you to say to me? You have been my enemy.'

'Only when you made your father yours,' William said. Nothing but honesty, he thought, would serve him now. 'As for our last meeting, I had it in my power to slay you, sire. Yet I only slew your horse.' He saw a sudden and appreciative gleam in the eyes above his and went on boldly, 'But if I had slain you I would not have committed a crime since my hands were set long ago between your father's and I served him while he lived. When I pay homage I keep my word.'

There was a moment's silence. 'And you will swear to

me?'

'I will.'

Richard set his hands over William's. 'I believe you, Marshal, your word is enough for me. And by God the two greatest warriors in Christendom should not oppose each other, eh? You will serve me as you served my brother and my father?'

'Life and living,' William repeated, and he thought, for good or ill, only please God for good, and Isabel.

Richard was about to proceed to the dais when he turned back to Geoffrey and said, 'I shall require the chancellor's seal, brother. You will not serve me in that office.' Seeing the reaction in Geoffrey's face he added, 'I shall make you my Archbishop of York. Will that please you? Aye, I thought it would. They made Becket priest and Archbishop on the same day and they can do the same for you – but you'll not set foot in England until it is done.'

For some reason they had never liked each other. Geoffrey was clever and popular and easy-going, none of which qualities was likely to endear him to his more severe half-brother, but though Geoffrey was clearly shaken by Richard's decree he now did a thing which was typical of his kindly nature. He bowed low and said, 'Your will shall be obeyed, sire, but I would ask one thing. Our father promised the heiress of Pembroke to William here. Will you honour that promise? William has given years of loyal service to your family.'

Richard paused while William waited, the experience a far worse moment than he had ever known in the height of battle. The new King never spoke hastily – still Richard Yea and Nay as Bertrand de Born had once called him – and then with one of those sudden bursts of generosity that he was renowned for and with a smile that bore no trace of rancour he said, 'Very well. Marshal, I will confirm all my father gave you – you may marry your heiress and rule her lands and you shall be Earl of Pembroke in her right.'

'Sire!' William rose. He saw now why men followed Richard; why, when the terrible seriousness lapsed for a few moments he became a man to command men, why they called him 'heart of a lion' in more ways than one. In the swift rush of his own relief and joy, the warmth of it spilled over towards the new King. 'You are generous, sire,' he said, 'and you will not find me ungrateful.'

'I am not such a fool as to throw away loyalty and valour when I find them,' Richard said succinctly. 'You shall do homage to my brother John for the Lady Isabel's Irish lands and take seizing of them when you may.'

John's rather full lips had drawn suddenly together but he inclined his head gracefully as if he shared the gesture. Perhaps he thought his tenure of the lordship of Ireland was no sinecure and it would be as well to have a man of William Marshal's calibre to keep order there. 'Very well,' he said indolently, 'but are we to stand here all evening talking? I would change my clothes – I am mud to the knees after that storm – and please God my father kept some passable cooks in this place.'

Richard looked him up and down and laughed. 'Go then, popinjay. William, come with me, my first commission for you will please you.'

He went up the spiral stair, climbing it two steps at a time and in the great chamber called for pages to bring water and fresh clothes, to ease him out of his mail tunic. For a while he talked of his plans, of his truce with Philip, their readiness to crusade together, of his coronation which must come first. 'And a look at my father's treasury in England,' he added. 'Please God there's enough there to fit out my soldiers.'

Will Longsword, of whom Richard was genuinely fond, held out the bowl for him while William held the towel. Richard washed his face and hands, rubbing his skin until it tingled and his red-gold beard until it was dry.

Will you to go England for me, Marshal? To my mother? Tell her she is free to go where she will, but I wish her to act as my Regent until I come for my crowning. Is that task to your liking? Ah, I thought it would be. I remember it was she who paid your ransom long ago, when the Count of Lusignan held you and I was only a child.'

William was surprised that he should remember, should on that account choose him to go to Eleanor with the welcome news. He tried to express his thanks but Richard cut him short. 'And while you are there, marry the Lady Isabel. You have my blessing and you may enjoy your marriage bed at your leisure until I come.'

'My thanks, sire, I had not expected –' William broke off. The prospect before him – in jeopardy so short a time ago – dazzled him so that he found it hard to keep his attention on the new King. Inadvertently he made an unfortunate blunder, for with a rare departure from his usual collected manner he went on, 'I trust your grace will soon have equal joy. The Princess Alice is in the castle, sire, in the bower no doubt –'

He saw Richard's face flood with angry colour, the blue eyes flash dangerously. 'That bitch! I'll not touch soiled goods. She shall be sent to suffer my mother's fate until I come to some arrangement with her brother – no doubt Philip will want her back, with her dowry. I don't wish to see her.'

William bowed at this outburst and laid the towel carefully on the table. Of course he should have known that all Richard's demands for his betrothed had in the past been no more than ploys in the perpetual fencing with his father. 'Your pardon, my lord, if I spoke inadvisedly. I meant no harm.'

Richard's anger evaporated. 'Yet not so inadvisedly, my friend, for a bride I will have. The King of Navarre is a friend to me and he has a daughter, the Lady Berengaria. She is little with dark hair like my mother had once.' He threw himself down on the bed, holding out his feet to a page who knelt with his shoes. 'Her eyes are black and her breasts small and her hands are beautiful. She looks at me as I think she looks at no other man.'

That was hardly surprising, William thought, for there were not many such golden young giants about, and it seemed to quash what he had always thought no more than ugly rumours, that Richard was guilty of great sin, of the preference for young boys to the company of the other sex. For the first time he felt at ease in Richard's presence. 'I understand, sir. My bride is also little and looks at me in that way, but her hair is yellow as Strongbow's was.'

'By God,' Richard said genially, 'we are fortunate, William.' He seemed to have forgotten the unfortunate allusion to Princess Alice. 'All men are not so blessed, I assure you. My cousin Philip has a son now but there was little to entice him to his bride's bed. I'm sure he had the candle blown out before he entered it.'

John had come in to hear these last words, his travelling clothes changed for shimmering green sendal, rings on his fingers and bracelets on his wrists. 'Well, there's always beauty to be found somewhere if not in one's own bed.'

'Aye, in the kitchens or the taverns with you,' his brother retorted good-humouredly. 'Well, get you to England, Marshal, to my mother. I'll give you a letter for her tomorrow.'

William sailed a few days later, his impatience such that

he thought he could not have borne a contrary wind. At Southampton his horses were brought ashore and with two knights, his squires and Jehan in attendance he rode the short distance to Winchester.

The news of her husband's death caused little change of expression in Queen Eleanor's face but it lit with radiance as she read her son's letter. Isabel stood behind her chair and in those few moments she and William exchanged glances of question and answer that brought an equal radiance to Isabel's.

Eleanor was near seventy now. The long dark hair Richard had spoken of was white, but she still had the imperious lift to her head, the regal dignity, though age and captivity, mild as it had been, had given her patience, a wisdom she had not had before.

She lifted her head at last. 'I am glad he sent you, Sir William,' she said and her eyes fell on the amethyst brooch. 'So you have kept that all these years?'

'Always, madame, to remind me that you saved my life.'

'I served our house better than I knew when I ransomed you,' she agreed, 'and now you are to have this dear child. We'll ride to London tomorrow and you shall be married in the chapel at Westminster Palace. After that we shall have feasting, you shall be given the best apartments. Perhaps a tourney can be arranged?'

'If your grace pleases –' William paused and held out his hand to Isabel who came to him. When he felt hers, small and warm in his own, he wondered how he had endured this whole year without her. 'All shall be as you say and we thank you for it except that –' he looked down at his bride's face, the deepening pink in her cheeks. It seemed to him she had matured during these long months, grown more of a woman and less of a child. 'Except that the brother of one of my knights, Sir Engerrard d'Abernon, holds the manor of Stoke near Guildford from Isabel's cousin, the Earl of Clare. He has generously suggested that as I hold no manor of my own as yet it should be at our disposal after the wedding. I have lived through a great deal since my young master died and I would rather my first days with my wife were spent quietly, away from the world.'

Eleanor was smiling as she listened to this speech and when he had finished she rose and kissed Isabel on the cheek. 'You are fortunate, my dear. Not many women find so loving and thoughtful a husband. Guard your love; it is a thing that fades and autumn can be a lonely time.'

And then, swiftly throwing off the moment of regret for things long gone, she picked up a steel mirror from the table and surveyed herself.

'Merciful Mary! Child, send for my women, for milk and unguents. When we ride to London I must look a Queen again.'

The little manor of Stoke was a delightful place set on a slope above the narrow meandering stream that boasted the name of the River Mole. The August days were warm, the banks bright with willow herb and yellow ragwort. The house was timbered and thatched, a comfortable unpretentious place, and the servants, overwhelmed by attending so famous a man and his lady, saw to it that everything was of the best for their guests. The hall was small but enough for their needs, the chamber above the west end reached by a single stair and catching the evening sun.

On the day of their arrival William found a new destrier stalled in the yard, a fine grey gelding well up to his weight and height. When he inquired where it had come from Isabel said demurely that it was her wedding gift to him. 'My father owed you a horse,' she said demurely, 'and I would not start my marriage with an unpaid debt on my conscience.'

William roared with laughter and named the animal Grisonné. When they rode out into the gentle Surrey countryside, hawks on their wrists, he commended her choice and she was forced to admit that Gilbert had gone to the horse market at Smithfield for her.

In the evenings they walked by the river watching the swifts diving over the water, the moorhens emerging from the rushes by the bank, and William forgot the long years of trial, of triumph and sorrow, of hard fighting and loneliness. At night, when they lay together in Sir Engerrard's bed, Isabel's small body folded within his, he knew a happiness he had not believed could exist. His experience of women was confined to those who made a profession of satisfying men's bodies and he had never guessed at the joy of a physical union that was enhanced by such love as had come to him and to Isabel. The fact that he was so many years older than she only added to his tenderness, to the delicacy of it all, but young as she was he taught her so deftly that soon her passion matched his own. Sometimes in the morning when he awoke early, as he had done all his life, he looked down at her, her sixteen years seeming less in sleep, the woman of last night becoming a child again in the dawn, and he would kiss her eyes, her hair, her cheeks, her mouth until she stirred and nestled sleepily into his arms.

The idyll lasted four weeks and then one evening Gilbert rode in to say that the King had landed and was riding to London for his coronation. 'It is to be the third day of September,' he added gloomily, 'a bad day – it has always been a day of ill-omen.'

But at supper he forgot his uneasiness and commended his young cousin on her looks, her pretty gown, her jewels, and surmised that wedlock suited her. 'As for you,' he said to William when she had retired up the stair, 'you look as satisfied as a young stallion.'

'I am content – as I think you are with Amicia?'

'Do you so?' Gilbert said drily. 'Well, Amicia is amiable and she bears healthy children and that's all I require of her. But you –' he studied William's face for a moment, puzzled at the expression there. Gilbert was settling into middle age though he was younger than William, his hair thinning, a paunch developing below his belt. His friend's rare happiness in marriage seemed to him an odd thing. He scratched his head and changed the subject. 'Have you heard who is to be our chancellor? No, I suppose you have not in this little Eden of yours. Well, there is a clerk in the chancellery at Rouen, a sly creature who calls himself William de Longchamp, though where he got that name God alone knows for it's said his parents were serfs.'

'Then why has Richard appointed him? I know he never has liked Geoffrey but Geoffrey knew his business.'

'Of course he did, while this fellow –' Gilbert gave a snort of disgust, 'he ferrets about, poking his nose into other men's affairs, snuffling into every deed. When the King goes to the Holy Land – and he thinks of nothing else – he believes Longchamp will keep everything running smoothly. The fellow's more likely to stir up trouble and he'd best keep his long nose out of my affairs.'

'I can't recall him.'

'Maybe not – you would not have noticed him. But if he is the kind of man Richard is going to appoint, God help us all – and England!' Gilbert finished and emptied his tankard of ale. 'Does this place boast a guest chamber, William, or am I to lie here in the hall tonight?'

William went to his own bed, somewhat disturbed by the news. His one hope was that Richard would be guided by his mother, for he heeded her and she had lost none of her ability to judge men. He held Isabel close, thinking that on the morrow they must leave this happy place, and it seemed to him that when he was old, if he forgot much else, he would remember Stoke d'Abernon in the warmth of August, the bright slopes and the little river, and Isabel in his arms.

King Richard's coronation was celebrated with all the usual magnificence but it ended with bloody violence that made it seem Gilbert had been right in his doubts about the choice of date. The King had apparently also been aware of the hesitation of his household and he had forbidden all witches or anyone who dabbled in magic to attend. The Earl of Essex, who considered himself something of a wit, asked behind his hand if it was because the King recalled his evil ancestress Melusine. The prohibition also extended to all Jews, for Richard had for them a hatred almost as great as his hatred of the infidels in Palestine, born of his passionate desire to make the Holy Places Christian again.

As he processed into the abbey, his sceptre was carried by the new Earl of Pembroke, his spurs by Sir John Marshal, the two brothers sharing the office of marshal and the elder, to his credit, showing no jealousy at his younger brother's prominence. He was mellowing with age and merely congratulated William on acquiring such vast properties by the hand of so young and pretty a wife. He commended his son John to William and William took the young man into his train of squires.

On this great day, bearing the golden sceptre behind the King, whose magnificent mantle of cloth of gold trailed behind him, William had a sudden flaring hope that despite Gilbert's gloomy prognostications Richard might become a great ruler of his inheritance. The ceremony was only disturbed by a bat which, escaping from the tower, flew round the coronation chair. Some men looked anxious and crossed themselves, de Mandeville whispered that perhaps it was Melusine in disguise, and the King merely looked amused.

The tragedy of the day did not occur until after the crowning, during the banquet. This was a wholly male affair; Richard had little time for women on such occasions and even his beloved mother feasted with her ladies, including the new Countess of Pembroke, in her own apartments.

While the long elaborate meal was in progress, the talk getting louder, the passing of jugs of ale and wine more frequent, William had a short encounter with the new chancellor. They were sitting opposite each other and to William he seemed almost a dwarf, staring at the world out of eyes that held no expression and seldom seemed to blink.

'I believe we have met before, my lord,' Longchamp said and William, taking an instant dislike to the man answered shortly that he did not recall it.

'Ah,' the chancellor's tone was smooth, 'you would not perhaps have noticed me then. I must acquaint myself with the new situation with regard to the taxes from the Pembrokeshire lands. As you know, the Exchequer is in need of every shilling due to it.'

The sheer effrontery of this momentarily bereft William of speech. Then he said, 'You will learn, sir, that I have been in the royal household long enough to understand such matters.'

'No doubt,' Longchamp agreed, 'but I have seldom found that longevity of service was any guarantee. Though,' he bowed slightly, 'in your case, my Lord, I am sure all is in order, and I will soon have everything to hand.' He took some bread, tearing it between thin fingers, his long velvet sleeves hanging awkwardly on ill-shaped shoulders. If he had been a horse, William thought contemptuously, he would have sent him away as worth nothing more than to pull a dray. But this man had been set in the shafts of England and he wondered with Gilbert what had possessed Richard.

It occurred to him then that for a little while there had seemed to be a growing noise outside and now it burst into a wild crescendo. All around the open spaces outside men and women were celebrating the crowning, milling about, many of them drunk, most very merry, but there was an ugly note about the sounds now and at a signal from the King the two marshals went out to see what was happening.

William caught sight of Walter d'Abernon in the doorway and asked if he knew. 'There's been a scuffle over there,' Walter told him, 'and some blood-letting. Jews, I think.'

'What are they doing here?' John Marshal demanded, 'I thought the King forbade them?' He tried to look over the scuffling mob but not being of his brother's height could see nothing. A fellow in the crowd turned and grinned obsequiously at the two noblemen emerging in all their finery from the feast. 'The stinking unbelievers thought that only meant they might not enter the church; they said they had come with gifts, but we didn't believe that. They plotted an attack on our new King, so we put a stop to it.' He grinned into William's face and a woman beside him screeched, 'Aye, they would have stuck a knife into his belly. See – they're paying for their treachery. Heathens! Scum!'

William pushed her aside and began to shoulder his way

forward, followed by his brother, his squire and several men-at-arms. Over the heads he could see that the centre of all his trouble was a circle of men and women yelling, screaming, kicking and beating some half-dozen Jews, dragging them by their long curled beards, seizing their gifts of gold and jewels and fighting over these. There was blood on the stones, one man had a broken head, another had blood running from his mouth, while a third lay groaning on the ground, clutching at his groin. The other three were in an equally bad way and William pushed his way through, his anger rising. But already the worst element in the crowd had done with these, and were shouting to the mob round them to follow to the city, towards Jewry, to burn the hated people out of their houses and out of the city.

William bent down and helped the man with the bleeding mouth to his feet.

'Ask him if he believes in our Lord Christ,' a butcher yelled. He had a meat knife in his hand. 'Ask him, my lord, ask him!' And he flourished his knife.

'I do – I swear it,' the Jew cried in terror and there was a howl of disbelief from the crowd. By now, however, more men-at-arms had come up and John Marshal ordered them to disperse the crowd while William and some others got the wounded and beaten men away.

Back in the hall the feast was still in progress, but on being told what had happened the King demanded to see the Jew who was leading the deputation.

Walter hauled him in front of the dais and William said, 'The crowd is out of hand, your grace, and what they are doing now in the city, God knows, but they were out for blood.'

'So I see.' Richard looked at the Jews one after the other and then back to the man who was trying to staunch the bleeding from his broken teeth. 'Did you plot to kill me?'

'No, sire – only to bring you gifts, to wish you well on this great day,' the Jew whispered. He was elderly and still shaking from the blows he had received.

Richard regarded him sternly. 'And do you believe Christ is the Messiah?'

The trembling ceased and the old man drew himself up. 'May the God of my fathers forgive me for saying it. No, sire, I hold the faith of my race.'

There was an ominous growl in the hall and the Earl of Chester called out, 'Hang him, sire, for such blasphemy. God's teeth, aren't we all going to fight to rid the world of such infidels?'

Richard paused, his wine cup halfway to his lips. Then he said. 'Release the fellow. He's had punishment enough and I may have need of him and his kind.'

The Jew and his companions were hustled away through a back door but when at last they dared to return to Jewry under cover of darkness they found nothing but dying fires and fallen roofs, and the charred bodies of their wives and children and they sat and wept amid the wreckage as their ancestors had once wept by the waters of Babylon.

'A bloody beginning,' John Marshal said. 'I like it not,' and for once William was in agreement with him.

He went and asked Richard what was to be done.

'Done?' the King queried and laughed. He was in a pleasant mood sitting among his courtiers with a lute on his knee, plucking at the strings. 'Why, nothing, Marshal, but to make them yield up their treasure for my enterprise. All England must yield up its treasure for me.' He glanced at William and his smile widened. 'I'll sell London itself if I can find anyone to buy it!'

The heat was beyond anything young John Marshal had ever encountered. The sweat rolled down his face and body, soaking his shirt and drawers, for he was wearing nothing else, and despite the wound in his arm, tied about with a bloody rag, he was swinging a pick with the rest of the men, regardless of the pain it caused.

Here in Ascalon on the coast of Syria, some forty miles from Jerusalem, the crusading army had marched last night, hot, tired and somewhat discouraged. The nights were as bitterly cold as the days were hot and John and his particular cronies, Robert de Beaumont, Leicester's son, Richard d'Abernon and his cousin William le Gras had built a fire and cooked the meagre portion of a kid that they shared with several others, eating hungrily and wrapped in their cloaks. This morning the herald had wakened them all at first light with his familiar cry of 'Help! Help for the Holy Sepulchre!' and now they laboured in the broiling sun to rebuild the walls of Ascalon which had fallen into disrepair.

At first the King rode round the defences. 'Everyone is to work,' he ordered, 'cooks and farriers and priests, all of you.' And shortly after he dismounted, stripped off his shirt and seizing a pick set about breaking stone to build up a breach. The sight of this giant King with the red-gold hair glistening in the sun labouring with his own hands cheered the men on and John thought, no wonder they follow him, no wonder they would all die here for him, which is what they might well do. He brought his pick down on a great rock and split it. It was his pride that he had something of his uncle William's great strength. His uncle had wanted to come on this tremendous expedition but the King had said firmly that he needed men he could trust at home and had made William one of his justiciars. John began to wonder what it would be like in England now, the meadows deep in buttercups, great pools of shade under the beeches, fields of green corn standing in the sunlight, cool streams meandering through the valleys. Sickness here had decimated the army, Baldwin, the Archbishop of Canterbury and Ranulf de Glanville among its first victims, and they all longed for a cool English breeze. Last winter there had been little to eat, but it was better now, even their enemy the great Sallah-ed-din sending baskets of fruit to his opponent, but none of that altered the fact that nothing was going to plan.

The English knights quarrelled with the French. 'When we have spent our lives fighting them,' de Beaumont said, 'it is not easy to find them on our side.'

One such quarrel had reverberated to the highest authority and Richard and Leopold of Austria had had a fierce altercation, so that when Conrad of Montferrat had been assassinated Leopold had gone so far as to hint that it might have been done not by Moslems but by two of Richard's men in disguise, and it was Leopold's minstrel who began circulating a vile and scurrilous song about Richard of England. To be slyly accused of sodomy was not amusing, particularly as it was whispered that Richard had done penance in Cyprus for 'grievous sin'. His minstrel Ambroise retaliated with equal mockery and the ill-feeling grew.

The English army as a whole loathed Leopold and his Austrians from that moment and now, pausing to lean on his pick and wipe the sweat from his face, John saw the Duke himself riding along to inspect the work. He paused where the King was heaving a broken stone into a gap. He said nothing, a supercilious look on his face, and Richard, turning to seize his pick again, saw him.

'In God's name, my lord Duke,' he said sharply, 'get down off your horse and help us.'

Leopold glared at him. 'I am neither carpenter nor stonemason, Richard of England – nor are you. This is no work for such as us.'

'Our Lord was a carpenter and it is for His sake we are here,' Richard retorted. 'Will you get down or do I pull you down?'

'Neither.' Leopold swore at him, flinging an obscenity at the man who stood tall enough to carry out his threat. 'You go beyond all, my lord. It is your arrogance that has undone us.'

'If anything has done that it is your cowardice and Philip's and Burgundy's' Richard retorted with truth. He raised his hand as if to carry out his threat. The contrast between himself, dirty and sweating, and the Duke in silks and jewels, was such that no one doubted the outcome, but Richard did not strike. Instead he brought his hand down hard on the horse's rump. 'Get you gone then – we want no man of your kidney with us.'

The horse, startled, reared and then went off at a gallop so that the angry Duke nearly came out of the saddle, swaying like a sack before catching hard at the reins to bring the horse under control again. The English labouring at the walls roared with laughter, but the next morning Leopold of Austria and his troops were gone.

'Good riddance,' Richard d'Abernon said cheerfully. 'The Austrians were worse than the French and God knows we've been better off without King Philip.'

'That bladder of lard!' John exclaimed. 'He's no soldier. A few months here soon sent him scurrying back to

France, and Burgundy after him, but will he keep the truce there? He's always sworn to take back the lands old King Henry took from him.'

'If he tries all Christendom will condemn him,' de Beaumont put in. 'Everyone is sworn by the Pope's order to protect Crusaders' lands.'

John gave an expressive shrug. 'I wonder if Prince John will remember that?'

'He wouldn't dare to challenge the King's authority, surely?' d'Abernon asked. 'He must have heard more than the bad news. Someone will have told him how we won at Arsouf, that the dead were piled like corn-swathes before the King. No one ever fought as he did then.'

'No.' The three of them began to walk towards the walls, the sun only just coming up, the heat not yet intense, the empty spaces where the Austrian tents had been littered with abandoned rubbish. John was thinking how far they had come since last year when they had feasted in Cyprus at the wedding of King Richard to Berengaria of Navarre, the last of comfort and luxury they had known. Though the new Queen and the King's sister Joanna, the widowed Queen of Sicily, had struck up a great friendship and followed them to the Holy Land, it was certain the King's mind was more on the war than on his bride. It was he who had persisted in the siege of Acre, reducing the garrison briskly enough and taking near three thousand prisoners.

'But men will remember Acre,' John said suddenly, and de Beaumont demanded to know why.

'Because we slew the prisoners? That was because Saladin did not keep his word to us about the exchange. And didn't we come here to slay unbelievers.'

'Of course,' John agreed. 'I don't care for the heathen –' yet it would be a long time before he forgot that day and the orders to kill and kill until not one of all that number lived, nor the screams and cries for mercy of those dark, terrified men. '– but I do care for Richard's honour, and because he would not wait Saladin slew all his Christian prisoners. We gained nothing.'

'Except that men learned to fear our King.'

They had reached the walls now, the Holy City lying so few miles away beyond those brown hills. 'Aye,' John said slowly, 'they do that.' The King's fighting strength, his skill in handling his men, in keeping this large army in the field so long, put heart into the meanest soldier. He was always in the forefront of any battle, flinging himself into every dangerous gap, so that his appearance anywhere was met with frenzied cheering. No wonder the other less capable leaders were jealous. Now Leopold too was gone and England faced the enemy alone.

All through the hot day they toiled and then Richard, considering the walls strong enough, called Hubert Walter to him. Walter, now Bishop of Salisbury, was as cool and careful as an army commander as he was as a cleric, a man very much after Richard's own heart and together they decided on the march towards Jerusalem.

'We will be there in three days,' Richard declared in ringing tones to his assembled troops, and the Bishop prayed in a loud voice, all men baring their heads, consecrating their efforts to God. It was a pity, John thought, that the army had to be followed by such a collection of pimps and prostitutes and such scum as were after any pickings that might be had. He was not above getting drunk himself and for most of them any woman was better than none, but the vice in the camp was at war with its ideals and he wished that Richard would forbid this mean and filthy tail to follow them. But Richard had his eyes on the road to the east and was oblivious of all else.

They halted at Emmaus where once Christ had revealed Himself and there the army waited as their leader and his chief officers conferred.

John and Richard d'Abernon were idly rolling dice when William le Gras joined them in the small tent they all shared, his face dark with distress.

'What is it?' John asked. 'God in heaven, what's happened?'

'We are to go back,' his cousin said and flung himself down on his pallet. 'They say we cannot besiege the Holy City. Now that the Austrians have gone we have not enough men and Richard says that the lie of the city makes it impossible as well as the disposition of Saladin's men.' He looked up at the two thunderstruck and disbelieving faces. 'Oh, it is true enough. We march back to Jaffa in the morning.'

John swept the dice aside in one impatient gesture. 'What have we come all this way for, then, if not to take Jerusalem?'

D'Abernon said slowly, 'Perhaps God is not with us. Our men fall sick and die every day, our allies desert us, and perhaps the King has offended –'

'Did we ever expect it would be easy?' John countered. 'The fewer the men the greater the glory and Richard has earned it alone for England.'

'I know – I know!' d'Abernon cried out in distress, his hands gripped together. 'But don't you see for some reason it is not right for us?'

'Well, I for one don't see.' Robert de Beaumont had come into the tent to hear the last words. 'I only know we had cowards for friends and the King has done all that any man could do. Why should God punish him for that? And you should have seen his face when he gave the order.'

John saw it next morning as the army led by Hubert Walter, his episcopal dress hidden beneath a coat of mail, began to wind its way back towards the coast. The King, usually in the van, rode with the rearguard this time, his eyes on his horse's neck, his shoulders bent.

A young knight came galloping up to him, all eagerness, his words tumbling out. 'Sire – Sire! If you ride up that low hill there you can see Jerusalem clearly. The sun is on the towers and minarets and –' he stopped, for Richard had raised his head and was looking at him yet without seeing him.

'The man who is not worthy to conquer the Holy City is not worthy to look upon it,' he said and his eyes filled with tears so that they spilled down his cheeks.

No one spoke. The knight fell back, abashed, and there was no sound on the desert road but the hooves against rough stone and the jingling of harness.

William was pacing a passage in the palace at Winchester, pausing occasionally to look out of the narrow window at the wintry landscape below, his mind on only one thing. There was much to occupy him but this morning state affairs were forgotten as Isabel laboured of their third child. His two sons William and Richard were with their nurse in the big house he had bought near Reading – Richard was an ailing child and it was thought best he should be kept quietly in the country – but Isabel had come here to be with Queen Eleanor when the news came that the King was missing.

His army, under Hubert Walter's expert command, was making its slow laborious way home, but Richard's ship appeared to have been wrecked on the Adriatic coast and the King himself had vanished – into an Austrian dungeon, some said, and William could well believe that

Leopold's hatred could sink to that. But no one knew for certain and Queen Eleanor's face was white and drawn with anxiety for her son, Isabel came at once to the Queen, though she was near her time, and now the child was to be born William waited outside the chamber in a fret of anxiety.

These two years since Richard had left England had been difficult ones for him. In the high office of justiciar he had clashed with both Longchamp and Prince John, though as far as the chancellor's behaviour was concerned he had been at one with the Prince. Longchamp's overbearing manner, his scorn of England and English law had finally gone beyond what could be tolerated, and when he had imprisoned the Archbishop of York, William's old friend Geoffrey, William joined the Prince in the storm of protest. Furious, Longchamp had excommunicated him, and a wretched uncomfortable time it had been, but the chancellor had overreached himself and Richard, hearing the news in Acre, had sent the Archbishop of Rouen, Walter of Coutances, to restore order. Longchamp was driven from the country, all Europe laughing outright at the tale of his attempt to escape in woman's clothing, only to be discovered at Dover by an over-attentive fisherman. The Archbishop rescinded the excommunication and now he, with William as his subordinate, ruled England in the King's name. William kept his eyes on Prince John, however. To his mind Richard had given too freely to that smiling, dangerous young man and there were too many French messengers arriving at Nottingham Castle, John's favourite residence. It seemed to him that John and Philip were playing as mice might play when the cat was out of the barn.

He began to pace again, his hands behind his back. The two births had not been difficult – for all her smallness

Isabel bore her children well – but there was always danger. So many women died in childbed and his love for Isabel grew daily so that he could not imagine life without her. He had been in the room for the birth of William, but he found it hard to watch Isabel's suffused, perspiring face, listen to her cries of pain, see her swollen body heaving beneath the coverlet. At least out here he could pray for her to the Blessed Virgin. He had lighted a dozen candles in the cathedral this morning when the pains came on her and now, at last, he heard the sound he had been straining to hear, a sudden thin wail.

It was over then, and a few moments later one of his wife's attendants came to the door. 'My lord, you have a daughter.'

'God be praised!' he pushed past her and went swiftly to the bed. Queen Eleanor sat on the far side, holding one of Isabel's limp hands, her own worry forgotten briefly in her joy for them. 'A fine child,' she said, smiling up at him, 'A daughter who favours you, I think.'

William knelt by the bed and took his wife's other hand, finding it hot and damp. He put it to his lips. 'My love –'

She gave a tired sigh. 'Are you sorry that it is a girl, my lord?'

'Sorry? Dear heart, we have two fine boys, it is time we had a daughter. She shall be well dowered and well married and our family will grow. Will it not be so, your grace?'

'If God wills,' Eleanor agreed, but the fleeting thought was in her mind that she had only two grandchildren, born of Constance whom she so disliked and who kept them, Eleanor and Arthur, far away in Brittany where she might not see them. But John was soon to marry and surely Richard and Berengaria would have children in the course of time. She was so fond of Berengaria and wished she could have comforted her in these days of anxiety. That Richard would not return she refused to countenance. Yet she felt old and dispirited today. She patted Isabel's hand and said she must sleep now, that William must see his daughter. He rose and bending kissed Isabel on the mouth, their tenderness for each other such that Eleanor felt an ache of envy for something that even in her most passionate days she had never known.

He looked down at his daughter. 'By all the Saints, she is indeed a Marshal, this little one.' He touched the soft crinkled cheek with one finger and then followed Eleanor from the room, filled with a sensation of completeness, of such happiness that he thought himself the most fortunate of men.

An hour later at supper that contentment was shattered by the arrival of an exhausted messenger to say that Prince John was in rebellion, that he had declared himself his brother's heir in the place of Arthur and that he had seized Windsor Castle. Eleanor's dark eyes flashed into life.

'By the Blood of Christ, is he mad? Has he proof that his brother is dead? No, I say! We will march at once, tomorrow morning, and lay siege to Windsor to bring him to his senses. My lord of Pembroke, will you order it?'

'Willingly, your grace,' he said at once. 'I promise you I will bring the Prince to terms and send you news as soon as –'

'Send?' she retorted. 'I am riding with you, William. Old I may be, but not too old to sit in the saddle. It is only two years since I journeyed to Italy with Richard's bride. I am not senile yet and it is I who will bring John to heel. He will learn that Richard's throne is not yet empty!'

She was utterly determined and together she and William with some six hundred knights set out for Basingstoke, sleeping the night there before pressing on to Windsor.

John held out for a while but the sight of his mother riding daily below the walls directing the siege operations unnerved him to such an extent that one night he slipped out of a postern gate. He retreated to Nottingham, the garrison capitulated and it was while the Queen and her followers were still there that William, standing one morning outside the chapel after Mass, looked towards the gateway to see a familiar figure ride in.

'Nephew!' he exclaimed and strode forward. 'What in the name of St Peter are you doing here?'

John dismounted. His skin was still burned brown from the desert sun, and he seemed to William to have grown broader and stronger. 'I bring good news,' he said at once, 'at least in part. King Richard is found. He is alive and in one of Duke Leopold's castles!'

'Thank God!' William seized his arm. 'How was he found? And is he free?'

John smiled, brushing the newly cultivated moustache on his upper lip, subconsciously copying his famous uncle in all things. 'It was the strangest affair. Do you recall that minstrel he had, Blondel, the fair fellow he used to sing with in the evenings? It was Blondel who found him by singing his way across Europe until he heard someone answer the song only he and Richard knew because they wrote it together. What a fellow! But,' his smile faded, 'the King is not free – though the news has caused such a stir that Duke Leopold is put out of countenance. Every ruler has protested that he should hold so great a warrior, especially after all that Richard has done in the Holy Land. He is forced to house the King better at least.'

'We must go to the Queen and tell her. But why has Leopold not freed the King? Surely now –'

'He wants a ransom,' John said. 'A hundred thousand marks.'

'Good God!' William exclaimed. 'How vile a man he must be – to hold a King of England who bears the Cross and trade for him as if he were in a market. Well, we will raise it somehow. Come, I'll take you to Queen Eleanor and you shall tell her it all.'

In Nottingham Castle John had also heard the news. A month later, despite the fact that his secret ally, King Philip, had offered to pay Leopold double the sum to keep his prisoner close, Eleanor and Richard's staunch supporters had begged, borrowed, raised taxes and somehow found the money. On hearing this Philip sent a brief note to John.

'Have a care for yourself. The devil is loose.'

Richard came home to a hero's welcome. William, however, had been summoned to the bedside of his dying brother and was not there to see it, but after he and his nephew had laid John Marshal to rest at Reading, they rode for London. William felt little grief. He and his brother had never been close and the younger John had always been more attached to his uncle than his father, and when they reached the capital they entered into the general rejoicing.

The bells rang, wine flowed in the streets, the people cheered themselves hoarse, and to his treacherous brother the King said no more than, 'You are a child and you behave as one but I forgive you. Do you still have your liking for salmon? I will have one prepared for you in a new manner I have learned that will delight you.' He laughed in a half indulgent, half contemptuous manner, setting an arm about John's shoulders, and William wondered that he could be so brilliant in the field and so blind in his judgement of men.

'Well?' Richard asked. 'What do you think of my "Saucy Castle", William? That will keep Philip from breaking my borders, will it not?'

They were standing high above the pleasant valley of Les Andelys where the river Seine turned sharply on a stony shore and a great rock jutted out some three hundred feet high, a vantage point Richard had been quick to seize on. The castle itself, walled and turretted, had been his own brain-child and day by day he had directed its building. William, seeing it for the first time, gazed about him in admiration.

'I can see it will prove a thorn in King Philip's side,' he said. The place was seething with men-at-arms, with the vast retinue of knights who accompanied the King everywhere, with serving men and cooks and butlers, fletchers and farriers and smiths, a small city in itself. 'I would like to know what King Philip thinks of it.'

Richard gave him a boyish grin. 'He boasted he would reduce it if the walls were made of iron – and I sent him a message that I would hold my Château Gaillard if it were made of butter.'

William laughed at this. But accustomed though he was to the interminable squabbles with France, he recognized that the bitterness that now lay between Richard and his onetime friend and ally was deep and lasting. They fought constantly along the border, seizing each other's castles, taking prisoners and ransoming knights, slaying lesser men with a brutality that seemed to William beyond the natural consequences of war. Even now in one of the towers Richard held the Bishop of Beauvais, a cousin of Philip's, and William was uneasy that he was still there in chains despite a temporary patched-up truce. He asked now if Richard intended to keep him mewed up. 'I fear it will cause trouble with the Holy Father,' he added.

Richard laughed again, but this time harshly. 'The bishop is fond of quoting scripture at me, but I say that they that take up the sword shall perish by it. I received the Pope's plea yesterday – for his son, as he called the bishop – and do you know my answer? I have sent his Holiness the bishop's mail coat, all bloodied from fighting against us. If he considers his bishops should put on armour to slay their Christian brothers then he is not fit to sit in St Peter's chair. No, the bishop will be ransomed as any other man taken in the field.'

'You are right,' William said, and then called out to his six-year-old son. 'William, do not climb up there.' The boy scampered down from the ramparts and came to his father's side. He was a large child, very like him, promising to have the same height and strength, and his father had recently betrothed him to the daughter of Baldwin of Bethune, a wealthy Norman lord.

'Sire.' He looked up at the King in awe. 'I have never seen such a castle. It will stand for ever, won't it?'

'I built it in that hope, Richard said, smiling. 'Go and see my friend Peter there; he is one of my stonemasons. Ask him to show you the highest turret, see, where my standard flies? He will make sure you don't tumble down.'

The young William ran off in high excitement and the King turned to his companion. 'You are fortunate to have so fine a son. And Richard, too – I trust you have named him as much for me as for Strongbow – does he keep well? You did say –'

'He is not strong, sire, but I think now he will reach manhood, he grows better with the years. Our third son, Gilbert, is a sturdy fellow and my lord of Clare stands godfather to his namesake.'

Richard turned to look out over the green countryside stretching away below them, and he gave a sudden deep sigh.

'I envy you, William. I have no heir of my body.'

William remained silent, watching him. Richard had wanted to marry Berengaria, perhaps in his own way he loved her, but he cared for other things more and neglected his Queen. She had never been to England and lived mainly in Anjou, seeing little of her energetic husband, who was constantly on the move, seldom at her side. William pitied her for on the rare occasions when he saw her she looked small and frail and sad. They were to join her in Aquitaine this Christmas and he guessed how she must be longing for the festive days to come. 'There is time yet,' he said, and Richard gave a shrug.

'Maybe – maybe. But this brings me to something I would say to you, William. If anything should befall me I do not want my crown to go to Constance's boy. For one thing my mother, who is like to live to be a hundred, could not tolerate it. Arthur is a sulky and ill-tempered lad and shows no sign of being the man to rule over England or Normandy, quite apart from my southern lands where they would not take kindly to a Breton lord.'

William hesitated. He knew England better than Richard, and John's temper, seemingly, better than his brother. 'Who then, sire? Prince John?'

'Aye, John. Oh, I know he is foolish and has little idea how to lead men, but if he has you and Hubert Walter beside him –'

'He is not far from thirty years old,' William broke in, 'and no green boy to be led. When you were in the Holy Land he listened to no one.'

'So I have heard. He behaved very ill and wanted nothing to slip through his greedy hands. But you will guide him, and he will be a better king for better men about him. You would not have Arthur?'

'God preserve us, no!' William said hastily. He had never

forgotten Constance's behaviour at Clare. 'And your mother would be horrified at the thought.'

Richard's face softened. 'If such a woman as she could rule it would be better than any King. Do you know that when I was in prison she signed her letters on my behalf to the Pope, "Eleanor, by the wrath of God, Queen of England". What a woman!'

'I have always known her greatness, sire. And she will hold your brother in check. I have often wondered what he thought when he looked down from the walls at Windsor to see her riding below. But please God you will reign many years yet.

'Pray then that God may hear you; I doubt if He hears me,' Richard said cryptically. 'He denied me Jerusalem. But I am a warrior, I'll die no other way. Come, let's go in to supper and I'll sing you my poem *"je nus hons pris"* which I wrote to while away my time in that cursed Austrian prison. It is a pretty tune – but I think you have little ear for music, eh, William?'

'None,' William agreed regretfully, and they went in together to the great hall.

At the entrance, however, Richard set a hand on his arm, a graver expression on his face. 'Remember what I have said. If you survive me, William, do I have your word that you will hold by my little brother?'

'You have it, sire, I swear it.' Yet even as he laid his hand briefly on his sword hilt, William thought of John, of that smiling face, heavier than the usual cast of Plantagenet features, the shifty eyes, the unpredictable temper, the total lack of judgement. But he had given his word.

Richard made him military commander of all the area about Rouen and he brought Isabel and the children to live in the castle there for he found it hard to be parted from her for long. In the summer of 1199 she gave birth to their sixth child and third daughter, whom he named after his mother's sister, Sybilla, wife to that Earl Patrick whose slaying had led to his imprisonment at Lusignan all those years ago. He watched over his growing family with pride and was already teaching the two elder boys the skills they would need as fighting men. William was an apt pupil and had an eye at the butts that sent his arrow straight to the mark. Richard, always less strong, was never able to compete with his elder brother, but he was never jealous and had a sweetness of disposition that endeared him to everyone. Under the care of John D'Erliegh he was learning to hold his own at least. Gilbert was inclined to live in a world of his own and to sulk if he did not get his way and William found him a trying child, but his godfather took his stubbornness as a sign of the mettle a warrior should possess.

'Let me have him when he is old enough to be my page,' Gilbert de Clare said and proposed that William's second daughter should be betrothed to his own son, another Gilbert. William agreed and the two children enjoyed the feasting though little Isabella had no idea why there should be so much singing and laughing and cups raised to her.

Shortly afterwards William marched out with a large company of knights to Vaudreuil where there had been a disturbance with some marauding Frenchmen. He settled the matter quickly enough and rolled into his bed to fall heavily asleep. In the small hours, however, he was roused by a knight who had galloped through the darkness to reach him and now shook him violently by the shoulder.

'My lord of Pembroke,' he cried out and his very tone filled William with a certainty of bad tidings. He shook the sleep out of his eyes and struggled up in bed. 'The

King?' he asked instinctively and reached out for his hose.

'Aye, my lord. An arrow, shot from the walls of Chaluz. It was only a small wound in the shoulder, not fatal, but –'

'Hold,' William said. 'Take your breath, boy, and tell me it all.' He had known Richard was at Chaluz. Some weeks ago a farmer, ploughing, had turned up a great treasure there, gold and silver, but when the King as overlord demanded it, the lord of Chaluz had lied, saying it was no more than a few old coins which were his property anyway. Furious, Richard marched on the castle. His need for money was pressing as always and such a treasure would augment his chests. Was this need, now, to be his undoing?

William reached for a costrel of wine that stood on the table beside him and held it out. 'Drink this and tell me –' and while the knight spoke he began to fling on his clothes.

'The surgeon took the arrowhead out,' the knight took a deep pull at the wine, 'but he made a poor bungling job of it, causing the King much pain, though his grace never made a sound, and now the wound is poisoned. The surgeon has tried everything, but the poison is spreading.' He paused and then, unable to restrain himself, burst into tears. 'He says the King is dying – and I wish the arrow had struck me, that I had died for him.'

William was pulling on his padded gambeson, leather shoes and long tunic, at the same time shouting for d'Erleigh to bring his arms. Could it be that the great warrior, the 'heart of a lion' had been felled like a tree with an axe set to it, that Richard who had survived so much was to be the victim of a lone archer? 'Did he send you to me?' he asked.

'Yes, my lord, but not to come to him – yet. He bids you

hurry back to Rouen to secure the city and the royal treasury for his brother John. I am to take your word back to him, but –' he brushed the tears away, 'but I fear – his mother is with him and Queen Berengaria and they did not think he would live – perhaps not even until I return.'

'Go at once then,' William urged him. 'Give him my promise, if he still lives.'

With the need for speed essential William took no more than a dozen knights with him and rode at once for the capital of Normandy, but he was scarcely inside the dark streets when a second messenger reached him, his own nephew John with the tidings of Richard's death.

In dying the King, ever generous, had pardoned the archer who had shot him – he had in fact applauded him at the time, deeming the wound trifling, the aim expert – but his grief-stricken and enraged followers had the man flayed alive, so that his tortured screams drowned the prayers of the priests over the dead King's corpse.

In grief for a man he had admired and respected, William prepared to meet the new King, the new Duke of Normandy. John! he thought. God help us all – and England too!

CHAPTER ELEVEN

The Countesses of Pembroke and Clare sat together and looked somewhat helplessly at the Queen of England who crouched on a window-seat in a most unregal fashion, her face blotched with crying, her reserve broken.

'I didn't know you cared so deeply for him,' Isabel said. 'Avice, don't weep – you will spoil your complexion.'

'Come.' Amicia leaned forward to take her sister's hand.

'Child, it is not the end of all things.'

'You don't understand,' Avice cried out. 'How can you? I have been a Queen, crowned, and now because John would have King Philip bound more closely to him, I am to be divorced so that he can marry that bitch of Angouleme.'

'You cannot blame her,' Isabel said quietly. 'She is no more than a child, not above thirteen years from what I hear. I am sorry, Avice, but perhaps the Holy Father –'

'He will do what John wants,' the Queen retorted pettishly, the tears momentarily dried by anger. 'John did not choose to remember when we were married that we shared a common grandfather, but it suits him now to ask that our marriage should be dissolved on those grounds. I shall be shamed before all the court.'

'You will not be shamed,' her sister said. 'You have done nothing to be shamed for and I would think it might be a relief for you. John can't have been the best of husbands. Gilbert says he boasts openly of his seductions, describes them when his attendants dress him in the morning, and as for that business with the Lord of Alnwick's wife –'

'Don't speak of it.' Avice clapped her hands over her ears. 'I know – of course I know, but a Queen has to bear these things and there were times –' she turned her head away and the tears came again.

'You told me once,' Isabel said, 'that when he came drunk to your bed he – he used such practices that –' she folded her lips tightly and then went on, 'I would have thought that more shaming.'

Avice's face burned and she raised her head. 'You – you and Amicia – you know nothing of men like John. But for all that I was his Queen and now I am to be nobody.'

Her sister touched her cheek. 'Never that, my dear. And you will wed again. Since Geoffrey of Mandeville came back from France I have noticed him looking fondly at you; it would not be too poor a thing to be Countess of Essex.'

The Queen, so soon to be dethroned, turned an even deeper colour. 'How can I think of another marriage? I can only think that a Frenchwoman, a child, will take my place. John will have her, he is determined although she is betrothed to Hugh of Lusignan, and I – I shall enter a nunnery.'

'Never!' Isabel laughed at her but in a kindly manner. 'You are not made for the cloister.'

Avice rose, the picture of pale outraged womanhood, and said mournfully, 'I shall ask your husband to write to the Holy Father for me. Everyone attends to William.'

'Better ask him to invite the Earl of Essex to dine with us,' Isabel said mischievously. She was in fact sorry for Avice, but she agreed with Amicia's sentiments, and wished that Avice could take life a little less earnestly. William had taught her to laugh at it. But her smile ended in a little sigh. She wanted to see him so much, but he was away in Normandy with the King; he was so important a man these days, always busy about state affairs, so often used as an ambassador to foreign courts because of his tact and his reputation. She wished she could have stayed in Rouen, but it seemed William sensed trouble and sent her home accordingly. Now she spent most of her time either at Pembroke or the Marshal manor at Caversham near Reading, or at Clare with Amicia. Only today all three of them were in her London home with its pleasant garden leading down to the river. It was probable that William was returning with the King and she wanted to be here if he did so.

But it was a brief visit for the King went back to France within a few weeks and married the Lady of Angouleme within a day or two of her impending union with Hugh of Lusignan. The marriage caused a storm throughout France but John cared nothing for that and when he brought his bride to England to be crowned he was inordinately proud of her. Young though she was she was developing fast, promising great beauty, with dark rippling hair and the manner of a coquette that was enslaving her much older husband.

Furious, Hugh issued a challenge to the King of England. 'Fool!' John said. 'Does he think a king can risk his life in single combat? Tell him to look for another woman for his bed. There are plenty for men of his degree.'

'Sire,' William told him, 'this will stir up trouble with King Philip.'

John gazed at Isabella who tilted her head, her smile full of secret allure, and it was doubtful whether he even heard.

'She is a witch,' Hubert Walter said in private to the Earl of Pembroke. 'She has bewitched our lord so that his thoughts are no longer his own.'

William, loving his own wife as he did, nevertheless saw something unpleasant in the way John behaved with his child bride, and he did not deny Walter's remark, but he had other business to discuss with the bishop. He wished to found a religious house where the souls of the Old King and of his former young master might be prayed for daily to the end of time. There was a stretch of land on a lonely part of the coast of Cumbria that had come to him from his wife. There, the bishop suggested, the monks might find solitude as well as caring for the needs of the few fishermen on that desolate coast. William agreed and put some of his great wealth into the building of a Priory at Cartmel for the Augustinian Canons. He would visit the brethren as soon as he might, but present events sent him hurrying back to Normandy in the King's train.

Rumour reached them that King Philip was on the march. Despite his outward friendship with John in earlier days, Philip was determined to seize back all that the Old King had won and a show of force was necessary on the Norman side. At Christmas at Caen, William with Gilbert and Will FitzHenry, now Earl of Salisbury in the right of his new wife, Ela, spent much of the time hunting the forests nearby. Riding through the snow-covered woods in search of game Will speared a boar. Watching while the men tied its feet to a pole to bear it back to the palace he blew on his cold fingers. 'Will you go further?' he asked his companions. 'I'll wager my brother will still be warm abed when we return.'

'We won't see him before dinner,' Gilbert agreed. He was puffing a little, his belly over-large these days and pressed against the pommel of his saddle. 'Holy God, his father could bed the old Queen and beget a son in one night and be off to the other end of his empire the next morning.'

'There will be no empire left if his grace does not exert himself,' William said. He leaned forward to take a fresh spear from d'Erleigh, having broken his in an endeavour to bring down a hart. 'My animal will be wounded and in the undergrowth somewhere. John, set the lyme-hounds to flush it out.' And when the huntsmen moved off, calling in their own peculiar way to the hounds, he added, able to speak freely to these two as he would to no one else, 'King Philip knows only too well what sort of man John is and he won't be slow to take advantage of it. The spring will see his banners unfurled.'

He was proved only too right, but for once John bestirred himself, perhaps because his mother was concerned. She was at Mirabeau and Philip, who had taken the cause of Arthur of Britanny under his wing, sent the sixteen-year-old boy with the Lusignans, still indignant over the matter of Hugh's stolen bride, to seize that stronghold.

'By Christ's Wounds,' John said, 'they shall regret the day they dared to hold my mother prisoner.'

In forty-eight hours he led his troops the eighty miles from Le Mans to Mirabeau and fell on the besiegers. William stormed under the barbican with picked knights and there was fierce fighting in the outer bailey. He had lost none of his skills and the years lay lightly on him, no fat on his body and his muscled right arm as strong as ever. He and his men drove the Breton troops to the closed gates of the inner bailey and there over a mound of corpses forced them to yield. And to his astonishment among the knights was a tall stripling, Arthur of Brittany. The boy wore a sulky look, his eyes dark with anger as he flung his sword at his captor's feet.

'Take it, William Marshal, and may God curse you.'

William signalled to John d'Erleigh to pick up the sword. 'He will not do so at your command, my lord,' he said, and John riding up gave a shout of triumph.

'By all the Saints, my lord Pembroke, here's a fine catch! Well, nephew, you have done very ill by me to besiege my mother. You will pay for this piece of folly.' He ordered his men to seize and chain Arthur fast and then with his barons beside him entered the gates now opened wide by the frightened garrison. Some twenty knights surrendered, including Hugh himself who looked at John with naked hatred.

Queen Eleanor was in the hall to greet her victorious son. She was eighty now, white-haired, her face lined, but she held herself proudly today, her eyes bright as they rested on the youngest of her brood.

They greeted each other with a kiss and then John said, 'Have they ill-treated you, my lady? While they held you have you suffered any discomfort? If so – '

'They have not,' she answered at once and looked keenly at him. 'I charge you, John, not to harm Arthur. He has used you treacherously, but he is your nephew, my own grandson.'

'I did not think you would care, considering how his bitch of a mother behaved to you,' John broke in and Eleanor flashed one look at him that reduced him to silence.

'Then you do not see beyond the end of your nose,' she retorted. 'Constance is less than nothing to me, but Arthur is a Plantagenet. Treat him well and perhaps he will learn where his best interests lie. He is still a boy. And as for Sir Hugh, you owe him a favour, you cannot deny that. It will not hurt you to be generous to him, and he has behaved towards me as a chivalrous knight should.'

John's lids were lowered. 'As you wish, madame,' he agreed in a silky voice. He signalled to his half-brother Salisbury to remove the prisoners and then in a different tone asked had the Bretons drunk all the wine in the place? He was knowledgeable about wine and during supper sampled enough that it was necessary afterwards for two of his attendants help him up the stairs to his bed where he sat laughing and hiccuping and demanding the prettiest maidservant to share it with him.

All John's needs having been supplied, William and Salisbury retired down the spiral stair to the small chamber seized on by Jehan for his lord. When the door was shut Will said, 'Do you think he will heed the Queen?'

William's face was grim. 'Only as long as she is beside him. But I heard her say at supper that she would like to journey south to Poitiers, her own city. She has been a great lady; I doubt there was ever a Queen like her.'

'I know,' Salisbury agreed. 'She was always kind to me

and to Geoffrey, and she had no reason to be so.'

In the morning Eleanor left, and it was Will who helped her into the saddle for she disdained a litter. 'Beg your brother to keep his word to me,' was her last injunction, but neither he nor William had much hope of it.

They marched north to Falaise with the prisoners and there John's young wife joined him and once more he lay in bed until noon. Arthur was well treated and given a large chamber. But the castellan of the castle, one Hubert de Burgh who was well known to William, confided to him that despite outward appearances he had doubts about the King's intentions towards Arthur and he was clearly uneasy about his own responsibility for the prisoner.

'Why?' William asked, though he shared those doubts. 'Has anything untoward occurred?'

'The King came to see him last night,' de Burgh said. He was an honest man, plain spoken and loyal to the royal house, a soldier born and not without ambition, but his eyes under his thatch of dark hair were troubled. 'The King spoke in smooth tones – you know how he does – asking Arthur to forget that he had any pretensions to the throne, but the boy cried out that he had a better right as his father was the elder brother.'

'No one can deny that,' William said slowly, 'If Geoffrey had not been killed in that tourney –'

'Aye, the matter would have been straightforward then, but mind you, my lord, I do not think Count Geoffrey would have sat well on the throne of England, and as for his lady –'

How Constance would have queened it over Eleanor, William thought, and there was no doubt Eleanor would have retaliated with vigour. 'I think I may thank Almighty God we escaped King Geoffrey and Queen Constance,' he said. 'And it was Richard's dying command that his brother should succeed him. He knew the naming of Arthur as his heir would cause worse feuding. What answer did the King make?'

'Oh, he strutted in front of the lad, all smiles, but he pointed out how high the tower was and how fast he held him. Arthur answered that nothing could frighten him into denying the rights he held from his father.'

'He has courage,' William admitted. 'Perhaps we might have made a king of him in time – but it is best as it is. I'm sure of that or I'd not have set my hands between John's.'

'I suppose you are right.' De Burgh took a long pull at his ale, a leather jug set between him and his companion. 'How fast your boys are growing – William seems set to be as tall as you. How large is your brood now?'

William smiled. 'I've had two other lads since Richard, Gilbert and Walter, and three girls. Matilda is to wed Hugh Bigod soon.'

'Your wife has served you well.' De Burgh paused for a moment, looking round the great hall, that hall where William the Conqueror had grown to manhood, dominating his barons from mere boyhood by sheer strength of personality. How he would have disapproved of John's licentiousness and indulgence at the table, he thought. He and William had sat down to a game of backgammon by the light of a rush dip, but most were extinguished now, the hall in semi-darkness, men rolled in their cloaks on straw pallets wherever they could find space. De Burgh looked closely at his companion's face and wished it was the Marshal who was in charge of the prisoner in the high tower instead of himself.

Presently William went to his chamber and there young Richard raised himself on his elbow. 'Father – is it very late?'

'Why aren't you asleep?' William asked, smiling down at the boy. From his own great strength he was always the more protective towards Richard, not despising the boy for his lack of physical attributes as some fighting men would have, nor packing the lad off to a monastery. Perhaps Richard would end his days in the habit but not yet, for he was not fully grown and he had the will to earn his knighthood which, to his father's mind, was more than half the way to it; bodily strength might yet come. He sat down on the edge of the bed they shared. 'I thought you would be tired after the hawking.'

It was the one sport the twelve-year-old Richard loved. 'It was good today,' he said and lay down again, looking up at his father. 'My new peregrine has learned to come back to the lure and she brought down a fine catch.'

'You have a knack with the birds. You excel your brother in that.'

'William hasn't the patience, but I wish I could pull his bow. I can hardly bend it at all.'

His father stood up and began to undress. 'William will be a warrior, but there are other things, my son.'

'I suppose there are,' Richard said sleepily, 'but mother wants us all to be like you.'

William gave a low laugh and got into bed, setting his arm about the boy's warm body. He wished other men had the joy out of their children that he had out of his. He thought of the Old King and the bitterness that had grown up between him and his sons, and he prayed that his own boys would not serve him thus. Young William was showing he could be headstrong; he was Salisbury's squire and eaten up with ambition to be a great jouster, to emulate his father who even now, in his fifties, no one had ever unseated, and William encouraged his son, teaching him as he had once taught the Young King and

Richard and Geoffrey and John. He thought of that other Plantagenet boy, only a few years older, barred in the room above, and wondered whether King John had any mercy in him.

'He has none,' Hubert de Burgh cried out some two weeks later, in answer to that unspoken question. He was nearly in tears. 'Jesu, my lord, what would you have done?'

'I don't know,' William said, 'but as God sees me I could not have obeyed the King.'

'Nor I.' De Burgh put his head in his hands, his fingers stuck deep in his hair. To blind the lad – hardly older than your William. And I'd grown fond of him. He stood firm against the King, even when he came drunk to the cell and taunted him.'

'Adversity has brought out the best in Arthur,' William gave a heavy sigh. It had been a grim business. Hearing those horrific orders – John in his crafty way realising that a blinded enemy was no enemy at all – Hubert de Burgh had refused to admit the King's men to the prince's cell and had given it out that he was dead in the hopes of saving his life. But this had caused such a commotion throughout France that the castellan lost his nerve, confessed, and brought his prisoner to the King at Rouen. Now Arthur was shut away in a cell there and de Burgh was in fear not only for Arthur's life but for his own.

'What shall I do?' he asked William. 'The King has said he is glad that no harm has come to the boy, that his men were exceeding his orders, but how can I believe him? The prince will die, my lord, I know it, and I can do nothing.'

'Please God you are wrong,' William said. But Arthur was close within the most remote cell in Rouen castle, a maze of hidden rooms as William knew from his previous command there. Now the castellan was one William de Braose, lord of Bramber Castle in Sussex, a bull-necked, loud-spoken man, a close companion of the King, and in William's opinion likely to stop at nothing to keep in favour.

For a while Arthur was forgotten in a clash with Philip of France, but a few weeks later John d'Erleigh came to William with a startling story. A fisherman, it seemed, had discovered a body in the Seine and reported it to a guard at the gates of the city. The guard had informed the lord of Bramber and the body was taken away for burial. The fisherman had been treated to supper by some of de Braose's men and had become violently ill, dying within a few hours of that fatal meal. It was whispered that he had been poisoned but de Braose denied it, calling the whole tale nonsense.

Salisbury went to his half-brother and asked plainly if the body had been that of their nephew Arthur, but was met with a blank stare and a pointed remark that Will must have other things to attend to.

'Jesu!' the Earl said to William, 'my father never resorted to secret murder to dispose of his enemies.'

'We have no proof that Arthur is dead,' William said.

'No, but do you doubt it?'

William did not, but the mystery remained. Men began to look even more warily at the new King and King Philip, judging accurately the character of his rival, marched into Normandy and seized that thorn in his flesh, Château Gaillard, while John lay in bed at Caen fondling his Queen.

William and the other commanders did what they could but without orders and without support it was a hopeless task. Remembering Richard's words William set out to try to relieve the beleaguered garrison in 'Saucy Castle' and wished with all his heart for a sight of Richard at the head of his troops. With all his faults the Lionheart knew how to make war.

There was fierce fighting with the French on the wet slippery rocks of the river bank, William's men charging with their cry of 'The Marshall, The Marshall' and for a while that name put sufficient fear into their enemies that they drove them back across the bridge. But there was no way they could reach the castle for the whole might of the French army about the rock outnumbered them ten to one. John promised to send supplies by ship, more mercenaries, more siege weapons, but none came and William, pale and angry, stalked his camp and stared up at the rock. Within were the remnants of the Norman garrison commanded by Roger de Lacey, but bravery alone was not enough to save them. De Lacey sent out the women and children for he had insufficient food and, trusting in French mercy, thought it more important to keep his own fighting men fed. The refugees tumbled down the hill towards the bridge, carrying pathetic bundles of belongings, but there the French drove them back. De Lacey refused to open the gates again and for two weeks two hundred of these women with their children crouched against the rocks, their cries haunting the English camp day and night.

'In God's name, are these knights engaged in war, or beasts?' William le Gras demanded of his uncle. 'And where is the King?'

William did not answer, only his fury rose. King Philip had won. He would take Château Gaillard and would win more, and William could see John losing all that his father had held. There was nothing for it but to retire, leaving the French victorious, and almost immediately the garrison capitulated. A few weeks later Philip took

Rouen, the capital. The loss of lower Normandy, due entirely to the folly of their lord, made William at least look back longingly to the days of King Henry. Beaten as he had been at the end that King had nevertheless held his empire and after him Eleanor had fought for it for her sons. Now, worn out with grieving for Richard, and despairing at the loss of his castle, Eleanor's strong spirit failed and in her own warm land of Aquitaine she surrendered to death. William mourned her deeply, left with an amethyst brooch and the memory of her kindness to a landless, penniless youth.

With her passing John lost all the sense of purpose she had endeavoured to instil into him, shrugged at the loss of Normandy and turned his eyes towards England.

'I tell you this,' Gilbert of Clare said tartly, 'we in England have no mind to waste men or money on John Softsword. He's no stomach for war and no sense, and every time he crosses the channel it is only to deny our laws, and bleed us all. It would be a blessing if he choked on his own spleen.'

William was in much the same mind but his strict code kept him silent. On John's orders he went with Salisbury to Philip to ask for terms but the French King eyed him coldly and only asked, 'Where is Arthur of Brittany?'

Neither William nor Salisbury could answer. The only concession they obtained from Philip was a personal one – a year in which to pay homage to him for their own lands in upper Normandy. William rode to Longueville and visited his steward, ensuring all was well there before returning to England. There he and Will reported the failure of their mission and asked John's permission to do the required homage. John seemed only half interested in what they were saying and gave a casual assent.

'Coward! Coward!' the words were flung at William.

'Poltroon, aye and traitor too!'

He stood his ground throughout the storm and when it subsided for a moment he faced the angry King and said carefully, 'Sire, you are unjust. No man has ever called me coward in all my life.'

'Coward you are! I say it again,' John shouted. His face was puffy and as red with fury as his marshal's was pale. His body had thickened now, the dark hair receding from his forehead, and his mood and tempers were even more uncertain.

They were in his chamber in the palace of Westminster and he sat in his carved chair, one foot thrust out, his fingers twisting his expensive jewelled belt, rings on his hands and a rich clasp fastening his mantle. Standing by him were his two closest friends, William de Braose and Randulph de Blundevill, Earl of Chester. De Blundevill had quarrelled with his wife Constance of Brittany and shut her up in one of her castles there, and he seemed unperturbed by the fate of his stepson, Arthur. Now he looked merely amused by the attack on the Marshal.

Hubert Walter was also there, standing by the window, and it was he who interposed now.

'Your grace, I beg you to consider. It will be of no avail to attack the French from Poitou. King Philip is too strong by far.'

'Your opinion was not asked for,' John interrupted rudely. 'You may have ridden to war once, my lord Bishop but you are old now and you give an old man's advice.'

'Sire!' William broke in. 'You have no cause to speak so to the bishop. He has served your house as I have, and have you forgotten it was he who got your brother's army home from Syria? We who fought under King Richard know –'

'Don't speak of him!' John banged his fist on the arm of

his chair. 'I know what you all think – you compare me with Richard. Richard! He thought of nothing but war, but I can be as good a man. I command you all to come with me into France and we will drive King Philip out of Normandy.'

'My lord, I cannot,' William said. 'I have sworn fealty to Philip for my lands.'

'Then you are a traitor.'

'But you yourself, sire, gave me leave – and Salisbury too.'

'I did not know you would act thus to my hurt – and as for giving leave, I don't recall I was so specific.'

If William had not been so disgusted he could have laughed at this. 'I assure you, sire, we had your word. You said that we might both set our hands between Philip's for –'

'Liar!' John spat the word at him. 'Do you recall my saying so in so many words, de Braose?'

The Lord of Bramber had been busy picking his teeth but he removed the stick from his mouth and said idly, 'No, sire, I do not.'

William gave him one sardonic glance. 'Fortunately we do not have to depend on the doubtful word of the late castellan of Rouen.' He had the satisfaction of seeing de Braose's face darken and went on, 'I am no liar, sire, as you well know and I am prepared to swear to your promise on the Holy Book or defend myself with my own body.'

'Aye, you'll do that,' John retorted bitterly, 'but you won't risk it against the French.'

'I'll not break my oath. I never broke it to your father or to your brothers and I will not go to war against my suzerain for the appointed time of my homage.'

Hubert Walter said in his tired voice, 'Consider, sire. My

lord of Pembroke is by all the laws of chivalry right in what he says, and I can only repeat my opinion that an expedition would be most hazardous at this moment.'

'It is for me to decide that.' The King glared at William and then added, 'Oh go – for God's sake, get out of my sight.'

William bowed. He felt for the first time the weight of his years. To be upbraided thus, after a lifetime's loyalty to the house of Plantagenet, was an insult hard to bear, but when he straightened he held himself stiffly erect. 'Will you give me leave then, sire, to go into Ireland? I have never yet visited my wife's inheritance and there has been trouble enough there that a strong hand would not come amiss.'

'Yes, go.' John indicated that de Braose should pour him some wine, which he drank off at one gulp. 'God's Blood, such arguing gives me a thirst, and I'll be glad to be free of your moralising. But hear this, Marshal, you shall leave your eldest son – nay, your two eldest – as hostages for your good behaviour. I'll have no man stabbing me in the back.'

'My Lord!' Hubert Walter was scandalised. 'My lord of Pembroke's reputation alone should assure you that he would never –'

'Hold your peace. Hostages I will have, and at once.'

William had stepped backwards involuntarily as the King rose and swept past him to the table where the wine jug stood and a bowl of fruit. He took a peach and began to suck it noisily, the juice dribbling down his chin.

William had both hands clasped behind his back, shaken for the first time in his life with real fear as he sought for the right words. What could he say? How could he leave William, and young Richard with his fresh face and eager ways, to the mercy of this volatile unreliable man about whom he knew too much? His feelings must have been naked in his face for the King went on spitefully, 'And since you are so lacking in trust of your King, I'll have that squire you are so attached to – what's his name, d'Erleigh? He can attend your boys.'

'Sire, I must protest –' William began, but fell silent again unwilling to anger John further, to rouse that venomous spirit to greater anger. The insults, the shame of false accusations mattered little compared to the safety of his children and, loath as he was to lose d'Erleigh, at least they would have a trusted friend with them. He glanced at Hubert Walter, seeing the Archbishop's face grey with fatigue and anxiety, and then, finding no words he dared speak and repressing the desire to strike the silly King who was now exchanging a joke with de Braose, he bowed with dignity and left the room.

The indignation of his friends, Gilbert, Will Longsword, his nephews John and le Gras, were as nothing to Isabel's reaction. When he broke the news in their chamber she became almost hysterical.

'My lord, how could you let him have them? Dear God, what has come to you? You know what he is – are you turned the coward he called you?'

'Isabel! You know it is not so.' The hurt at her words was submerged in concern as he tried to take her in his arms, but her body was rigid, her hands clenched. 'He will not dare to harm them.'

'After what he did to his own nephew?'

'We do not know – '

'Oh!' she raised her fists against his chest in impotent grief and fury. 'William, you cannot be so blind. Of course we know – all Christendom knows. Arthur is dead, murdered by that dreadful man, de Braose, or by the King himself. You know John d'Erleigh said he had spoken to a squire who swore that he saw the King come from the tower at Rouen with blood on his hands. Everyone knows at least that he was guilty of ordering it – and you will leave our boys with him!'

'He has other hostages for good behaviour. Windsor is full of children he holds for lords of lesser degree than myself, and he dare not antagonise us all. There is resentment against him in England as it is.'

'He is crazy enough to dare anything to get his own way.' Suddenly her rigidity collapsed and she sank against her husband, sobbing, her face pressed into his chest 'We will never see them again, I know it.'

'Of course we will.' He spoke with a confidence he was far from feeling and the hand which he put up to smooth her hair shook, his other arm closing about her shoulders. 'My love, my dear heart, do you think I don't feel as you? But what are we to do? We must trust to Hubert Walter and to Gilbert and others of our friends to keep a watchful eye on the boys. And d'Erleigh would let himself be torn in pieces before he allowed anything happen to them.'

'Do you think the King would hesitate to slay John if the mood was on him? Oh, William, William, I am afraid.'

He held her close, not knowing how to comfort her, and for a while they stayed locked in each other's arms. He thought of his other boys, of Gilbert, whom he cared for least, who because of his dislike of the martial training had now left his godfather's service and entered the schools in Paris where he might take minor orders, of Walter who was still young enough to be at home at Pembroke but was growing up sturdily and showing signs of wanting to follow in his father's footsteps – at least Gilbert was safe and Walter he would take to Ireland with his daughters. Matilda had developed into a pretty girl with pleasing manners and was utterly devoted to her father and the thought of her brought a warm glow to William's face. She was the delight of his life and he had recently betrothed her to Hugh Bigod, whom he liked. He would not for any material reason have given this darling child to any man he did not trust. Isabella had long been promised to Gilbert's son, and Sybilla to Earl Ferrers' eldest boy, good marriages which should secure their future. He had reason to be proud of his growing family and his hopes for William and Richard were lacerated by the King's decree. To imagine them held at the will of the unstable John was a picture he could not shut from his mind, nor could he forget his last sight of the seventeen-year-old Arthur of Brittany, chained and threatened, nor Hubert de Burgh's horrifying story. And what worse thing had befallen Arthur before he died?

Isabel was still sobbing but quietly now. As if she had read his thoughts she gasped out, 'They will disappear as Arthur did. Don't you see – you have destroyed them by your pride. Why couldn't you do what John wanted? What does King Philip matter? He was always our enemy.'

William stood stiffly, his arms still about her. 'He does not matter, but my word does. All men know that once given I keep it. Should I sacrifice my honour now?'

'To save our children? Yes!'

'I do not know that it would, nor that we shall lose them if I keep it. But I have no choice.'

Her sobs broke out again. 'You have – you have – only you are too proud.'

He gave a heavy sigh. 'Isabel, you do not understand. My love for William and Richard is not in question, you know that, but my honour is and I will not break my word.'

She struggled free of him and stumbled away to the bed where she sank down clinging to the bed post. 'It is you who do not understand. The lives of our children are all that matters, and you will give them to that devil. They say he never goes to the Sacraments, he cares nothing for God and His Holy church. Why should he care if he murders? They were all devils – all the princes of Anjou.'

He stayed where he was, not attempting to go to her. 'Not as John is. The Old King and my own master would not have acted as John has.'

She made an impatient gesture. 'Then why – ?'

'He is the King,' William said and did not know how stern he sounded. 'He is the King, Isabel.'

For a moment there was a bleak silence, an immeasurable distance seeming to separate them. Then he crossed the mere yard that it was and stood above her though he did not touch her. There were tears in his own eyes now. 'Dear love,' he said, 'we have had so much joy together – don't let this separate us now.'

His quiet voice, all the severity gone, reached out to her and rising she went once more into the security of his arms. 'Forgive me, forgive me, my lord. When all is said it is you who are my heart, my life. We will pray together, to Our Blessed Lady – she will keep them safe.'

'Aye,' he said, 'safe –' and thought, even if 'safe' should mean out of this wretched world where men such as John could wield such power over men's lives. But he did not speak the words. Instead he bent to kiss her mouth and as she raised her arms to entwine them about his neck he thought suddenly of Stoke d'Abernon and the little river and those golden summer days. If sorrow came to them now, there had been joy before, and both would bring them closer together than at the untried beginning. And later, when they knelt together in the light of candles before a statue of the Blessed Virgin in the chapel, his petitions for his children were mingled with thanksgiving for the gift of such a wife.

CHAPTER TWELVE

Mountainous waves hurling themselves against the ship drove Isabel into the small cabin, her children and attendants crowded in with her, Joanna clinging to her mother's knees and the baby Anselm crying loudly. The Irish Sea heaved and fell and the sailors, expecting every moment, to be hurled into the angry waters, clung to the ropes gabbling their prayers, hardly able to hear the orders of the captain. He stood with the Earl of Pembroke, both holding fast to the mast, the wind driving the spray at them until they were soaked to the skin. William's cloak blew out behind him and his hood from his grey head so that the hair was plastered to his forehead.

'How much longer?' he called out against the noise of the wind and the sea.

'About half an hour, God willing,' the captain shouted back, 'That is, if we can make harbour.'

They were bound for Milford Haven, the weather calm enough when they had sailed from Wexford, but this storm had blown up during the night and now seemed likely to engulf them all.

'God and His Saints preserve us,' William said and the captain gave an amen to that, adding, 'I've seen worse and come through it, my lord, but I'm sorry for your lady and the little ones. Hold, you there! Mind that sheet.'

Clinging to whatever came to hand, William left him to his task and made his way to the cabin set aft. There he found Isabel seated on a stool, Joanna in her arms, while the wet-nurse, her rosy Irish face pale now with terror, suckled the baby in an attempt to quiet him. Jehan, old and grizzled but as faithful as ever, was holding Walter's head over a basin, and the other two girls, Sybilla who was ten and the eight-year-old Eva, clung together, the elder trying to comfort the younger whose face was wet with tears.

'Come now, 'William said cheerfully, 'the captain tells me we shall soon be in port and then our own barge will take us home to Pembroke.'

'Home!' Isabel exclaimed and raised her head. 'It has not been that for a long time.'

'I know.' The ship gave a violent lurch, Joanna howled and Isabel steadied herself against the wall as Jehan and Walter tumbled together to the floor. William picked up the sick boy while Jehan found a cloth to clean up the mess. 'There, child, you will be better soon,' he added as Walter, exhausted, lay against his father's shoulder, his stomach still heaving.

'Jesu!' William gave Isabel a reassuring smile. 'What a crossing. I've never known it so before.'

Isabel looked up at him out of tired eyes, enlarged by her desperate anxiety. 'It is the curse – I know it. You remember?'

'Of course I remember,' he answered rather shortly, 'but it was nonsense. God does not attend to the mouthings of a tiresome old man, even though he be a bishop. Our Blessed Lady will bring us safe home.' But he spoke with rather more confidence than he felt as the wind buffeted the straining timbers.

These last years in Ireland had been a mixture of pleasure and annoyance. In many ways William had been glad to be out of England. Hubert Walter had died nearly eight years ago, shortly after he had been forced to give William and Richard as hostages, and the King had crossed swords with the Pope over the election of a new Archbishop of Canterbury. The quarrel had come to such a pitch that it brought England under Interdict. Innocent III set aside John's choice of his friend the Bishop of Norwich as well as the monks of Canterbury's own choice of one of their brethren, and determined that Stephen Langton, a brilliant and scholarly Englishman, should sit in Augustine's chair. John did not like Langton and swore to hang him if he set foot in England and Langton remained at Pontigny where so many years ago, William remembered, Thomas Becket had sheltered from King Henry's wrath.

So the church doors were locked, bells taken down from steeples, images covered with purple cloths and the people denied the familiar rites of baptism, marriage and burial with funeral candles and holy water. A terror lay over the land but John thumbed his nose at the Italian Legate. He had never cared for the Church, made sacrilegious jokes and threatened to give any man sent by the Pope to his torturers for their pleasure.

Spending most of his time in Ireland William had been free of the horror of the Interdict. On one visit to England, seeing the misery of the people, the desperate plight of the clergy whom John now cheerfully robbed of their revenues, he had besought the King to come to terms but was told he was becoming addled in his old age.

He returned to Leinster where he had his hands full. For the most part his wise rule had kept peace in that turbulent country, but he and the Bishop of Ferns had quarrelled over some land and the Bishop took up arms against him. William promptly sacked Ferns itself, though he permitted no outrage against the monks, and then the Bishop, his white beard reaching his waist, cursed William Marshal, prophesying that for this blasphemous act his line would die, none of his sons begetting sons of their own. William had listened to such outbursts from defeated enemies before, but the Irish were a strange people, the memories of old cults, old gods, still half alive, and when the Bishop followed his Christian curse with another in a language William did not understand, holding a branch of a rowan tree in one hand and a sprig of mistletoe in the other, he was stirred into a certain uneasiness.

Isabel had been plainly frightened and he had told her to pay no heed to such superstition, but now in this heaving ship, sounding for all as if it was in its death throes, he began to wonder if there was indeed a curse, if he and all his younger children were to perish. At least William and Richard had come to no harm, though he remembered with private alarm the fate of the lord of Bramber's son. William de Braose had fallen out of favour with the King and fled to Ireland with a nauseating tale. It seemed that John in his usual way had demanded de Braose's son as a hostage, and though de Braose would have yielded his lady was of sterner stuff and refused to hand over the boy to the King's messengers. John then took both mother and son by force, thrust them into a cell and had it barred. When it was opened nine days later they were both dead, the child's cheeks gnawed by his starving mother.

De Braose, tough and hardened though he was, wept and raged when he told the story. William was appalled, pitying de Braose though he disliked the man, and he could think of little but that his own boys were in John's wilful hands. Fortunately John had been busying himself by founding a city which he named Liverpool, interesting himself in architecture, and he was by all accounts still infatuated with his Queen who had given him two sons and three daughters. Nevertheless William was impatient to be at home.

The ship was quieter now, the heaving more gentle. William had one arm about Isabel's plump body, the other still holding Walter who had fallen asleep at last, and when a sailor appeared at the door to say that the ship would dock shortly he turned to his wife with a swift smile.

'So much for the Bishop's curse, my heart. We're all come safe through.'

She leaned her head against his shoulder. 'God be thanked. I would not have feared to die with you, William – but not to see our little ones perish too.'

He closed his eyes momentarily, his cheek against her hair, and thought of the great fire in the hall at Pembroke Castle, the hot food, the bed where he and Isabel would sleep, the children close by, and he dismissed from his mind the wild mutterings of an old Irishman.

King John was at Windsor when William rode to meet him. He knelt, setting his hands between the King's and it seemed to him that John had aged, that the long years of quarrelling with the Pope in the face of the opposition of all Christendom had taken their toll of him – though no doubt it was his self-indulgence at the table that had set that great stomach on him.

He seemed to be in a jolly mood and welcomed William warmly. 'You have served us well in Ireland, my lord, and now we have need of you here. But first I return your sons to you.' He beckoned and William rose quickly as his firstborn, now a tall, well-built young man of twenty-two, came forward, kneeling for his father's blessing. William raised him and embraced him, seeing himself as he had been more than forty years ago. He had heard from his friends of the younger William's success at tourneys, developing great skill at arms, but what was more surprising was that Richard, coming forward to greet him, had outgrown all his early ill health and was now only a little less tall and strong than his elder brother. He had become very like Strongbow and William folded him in his arms, scarcely able to keep tears of joy from his eyes. He turned back to John. 'I thank your grace for your care of my sons. They are life to me.'

'And here is mine,' John said. He set an arm about a boy of six, with the familiar Plantagenet hair and something of his mother's striking beauty, his only defect a slight drooping of his left eyelid. 'Henry shall be put in your charge, my lord, and you shall teach him as you taught me. How will you like that, my son?'

'Oh very well,' the prince agreed, but looking up at the tall Marshal his expression became a little doubtful. 'That is if my lord of Pembroke is not too old for such a task?'

There was a roar of laughter from the assembled court and William answered amusedly, 'I think, your grace, I can still bear a sword well enough to teach you how to use it.' The boy had flushed with embarrassment and he added, 'We will go out together tomorrow and you will find out how old I am become!'

John, whose sense of humour seldom deserted him even if occasionally it took a macabre turn, was highly amused. 'If you tell me, Henry, that my lord here cannot match you, perhaps I must put you in charge of my army!' Then his expression changed sharply and he began to fiddle with a jewel about his neck. 'You have heard the latest news from France, William? No? You will soon understand why I have sent for you. It seems that the Pope has dared – dared – to offer my crown to Philip of France. By God's Teeth, it is beyond bearing. I shall slit Philip's nose for him if he sets foot on my land. He will find the blood of the Conqueror in me yet.'

'I doubt,' William said carefully, seeing the humour vanishing and all the signs of rising Plantagenet rage, 'that the King of France would try to cross the channel. What measures have been taken?'

'Ah, for once my barons are behind me,' John retorted sarcastically. 'All along the south coast they are assembling the levies and if Philip thinks to emulate my ancestor he will find that I am no Harold to be caught napping. You will see!' He rubbed his hands together, glancing round the hall. 'That is why I have sent for you, my lord – for all of you. I need every able commander that I have.'

A conference was held at once and it was much later that night that, in the private chamber put at his disposal, William was able to talk with his sons and with John d'Erleigh to whom he now felt he owed so much. He conferred on his faithful squire a manor in Berkshire and offered to knight him, but d'Erleigh refused this, though he accepted the manor. He had, he said, a mind to marry but none to quit his position as squire to his lord. They all three told him of much that had been happening during his absence and when he inquired after the Earl of Salisbury heard that he had taken a fleet of ships to sea in the channel to chase the French away.

'Will always did like the sea,' he said and glancing at his sons added, 'I think it will be many a day before I can induce your mother to board a ship again.'

It was a happy reunion but presently into their talk came all the indications William had feared – the escalating of the terrifying Interdict, the discontent, the number of barons who had very real cause to turn against the King, John's unscrupulous methods of amassing gold, indeed Richard said it was common knowledge that the King had his men extract the teeth of reluctant Jews, one by one, until they yielded up their treasure to him.

He is a monster at times,' his elder brother agreed. 'I tell you, father, we feared for our lives when he turned against the lord of Bramber and shut his lady and their son into that cell –'

'Don't talk of it,' William said and his eyes rested on first one and then the other. 'I swear I will build another holy house, such as Cartmel, as a thanksgiving for your safety as well as your mother's and mine. On board that ship I feared it was we who would not see you again in this world.'

In celebration the younger William was married at last to the Lady Alice of Bethune and at a lavish feast the King made equally lavish gifts to the young couple. A joust was held as part of the celebrations in which the bridegroom rode against his father and after a splendid display which delighted the court, the honours were declared to be even. William laughed and set an arm about Prince Henry's shoulders. 'The old war-horse is not done yet, eh, my lord?'

The boy looked up at him in undisguised admiration, 'How many tournaments have you fought in, my lord?'

William scratched his cheek thoughtfully. 'I cannot remember the number, but it must be near five hundred.'

'Were you often unhorsed?'

'Never,' William told him and from that moment the young Prince was constantly at his side.

But this brief interlude of peace and goodwill lasted only a short while. King Philip of France, scheming for his son's future, and on fire to carry out his threat made so long ago under the tree at Gisors, assembled a huge army on the coast of France. Despite the fact that the Earl of Salisbury had soundly defeated his fleet at sea, he prepared confidently, with the Pope's blessing, to invade and conquer England.

John, on hearing this, yielded to sheer temper. Foam flecked his mouth, he screamed and flung himself on the floor and his attendants could neither hold nor calm him. The next day, to the utter astonishment of his councillors, he capitulated. He would yield to the Pope, make every concession, Cardinal Stephen Langton should come home to his archbishopric, and England should become a fief of the Vatican.

'God in Heaven!' Gilbert de Clare exploded. 'England a fief? Never while I live – nor a hundred others.'

'What can we do?' William demanded. 'We cannot go on thus with our churches locked and barred. Since I came home I have learned a great deal. The King must be stopped from this sacrilegious robbing of God's Church. A man who can treat His priests as John has done is in danger of his immortal soul.'

'You cannot mean you want this – this grovelling surrender?'

'I do not. The King has gone too far, but the Archbishop is no fool and we will get better terms in time.'

'Then you are more sanguine than I am,' Gilbert said. 'The barons will not stand for John's madness much longer.'

William was used to Gilbert's outbursts, but as time went by he became aware that the deep-seated resentment was gaining menacing proportions, and in due course a group of noblemen and knights gathered to put their grievances to the King.

'Rebels! Cowards!' John jeered, 'Find out what they want, William.'

So he rode out, attended by Richard and John d'Erleigh, to meet them at Brackley and there encountered first his eldest son. 'William! I did not think to see you here.'

The younger William stood beside his horse, a hand on the stirrup leather, his face grave. 'I wish, my lord, we had you with us.'

'Do you?' his father queried. 'I am the King's man as you should well know.'

'After all he has done? For God's love, father, consider. Is he the man King Henry was? Or even King Richard. You have told me enough for me to see that he is not. He has lost Normandy for us and will destroy England if we do not act. Because he gave me a wedding gift that does not mean I can forget all the men he has cheated and slain, nor my lord of Bramber's wife and son! How can you uphold him?'

William had listened in silence to this impassioned speech and when he answered his voice was stern. 'It is you who do not understand. It is not the man but the crown that matters. I have sworn to John as King and while he sits on England's throne, he has my loyalty.'

'And if he had murdered Richard and me as he murdered Arthur? Father, if you stay with him you will be our enemy too.'

William stared down at his son, seeing the uncompromising eager vitality of youth, remembering himself as he had been at that age, entering the lists at Boulogne with everything to gain, while by his side Richard, who had been silent so far, cried out, 'William, you cannot mean that. You would not turn your sword against our father? If you did,' his face suffused with colour, 'by Christ's Blood, I would slay you myself.'

His brother laughed. 'Would you, cockerel? It is I would slay you, I think.'

'Peace! Peace!' their father broke in. 'I'll not have quarrelling between us. William is, I suppose, following his conscience and so am I. The King has sent me to find out what is asked of him and this I must know.' He glanced round the field, bright with early buttercups, the sunshine warm, the oak trees casting great shadows, the men gathered in groups, a few standing foremost, waiting to speak to him. 'Well, messires?'

His son said, 'Come to my lord de Vescy and Sir Robert Fitzwalter. They will act as our spokesmen.'

William dismounted, throwing his reins to John d'Erleigh. De Vescy of Alnwick and Fitzwalter, he thought, were two men deeply injured by John in the matter of one's wife and the other's daughter, and their hatred was predictable, but the strength and truth of their statements impressed him. The rights of the Church were to be safeguarded, the old laws of King Henry I concerning land, inheritance, the disposal of widows and heiresses to be respected, the cities to have their ancient freedoms, the powers of the sheriffs and constables to be clearly laid down.

Fitzwalter, a small wiry man in his forties, finished the list and stood in silence facing the Marshal. He was very much in awe of this famous man with his dignified bearing, his long slit tunic of red and green matching his shield of the same ground bearing the golden lion of his office, but he had no fear for the Marshal's honourable dealings were too well known for that. Eustace de Vescy, however, was less respectful; his violent temper was renowned. He pushed past Fitzwalter and shouted, 'Tell the King our conditions, my lord Pembroke. Omit nothing, for be sure we mean every word of it. We've had enough of John Softsword's treachery.'

William stared haughtily at the angry red-haired Northumbrian. 'He shall hear it all, my lord. If the matter can be conducted without raised voices and violence it will be better done.'

De Vescy subsided, muttering, 'Well, see that he knows we mean it.'

'He will say that you are traitors all, though I will tell him your demands are reasonable enough.'

'We are true to England and our old laws,' someone in the crowd called out and there was an outbreak of voices giving approval, the murmur growing to a mixture of cheering and added exhortation.

William held up his hand, and such was his authority that silence fell within a few moments. 'I will do as you wish,' he said, 'but I implore you, all of you, do not plunge our land into civil war before I have spoken to the King. Our swords may be needed elsewhere.'

'You are right,' Fitzwalter agreed, 'and we thank you, my lord Marshal, for coming to us.'

'They thanked you!' the King exclaimed with scorn when William returned to him. 'It seems they care more nicely for you than for their King. They have no word for me but *demands – demands!* Jesu!'

But rant as he might, on the advice of Stephen Langton, of the papal Legate Pandulfo and of both William and his old friend Amaury, now Grand Master of the Knights Templar, he yielded. On Monday the fifteenth day of June in the year 1215 he rode out of Windsor Castle to a meadow called the Running Meade by the river Thames. There, with pitifully few attendants for a King, he made his way to where a small pavilion had been set up for him that he might be shaded from the sun.

The increased numbers of his enemies assembled on the greensward appalled him and he could see the banners that told him that nearly every great house was against him. Fluttering in the light breeze he saw the colours of Bohun and Mowbray, of Marshal's son-in-law Bigod of

Norfolk; the Percy was there and de Lacy, the wealthy Earl of Essex who had married Avice his discarded first wife. William de Ferrars, betrothed to another of William's daughters, bore his pennon high on his lance as if to flaunt it beside de Vere and Mortimer, and several marcher lords had brought large retinues, so that it seemed as if all England was there to confront their King.

Dully, John listened. The long articles of the Great Charter were read out, and when it was laid before him he picked up the quill and his hand shook.

In that long moment of silence, while every man waited, William glanced at Will standing beside him, their old friendship binding them together as always. But he could see many other friends on the other side, among them Gilbert de Clare and his son, his own son William, his sons-in-law, as well as several barons related to the King. John Marshal, in his place as always beside his uncle, muttered a curse on those who divided a family in two, but whether it was meant for his cousins, the rebel barons or the King, William did not know.

Salisbury raised one eyebrow and gave a faint shrug, a frown of deepening anxiety on his face. He had little personal liking for his half-brother, but an intense loyalty to the family who had accepted him, bastard as he was.

At last, when men had begun to shift their feet and glance at each other, the more impatient muttering among themselves, the quill descended and the name JOHN was written at the end of the parchment while the clerk busied himself setting the great seal to it. There was a resounding yell of triumph from the assembled barons as John rose. He gave them one cold look, and remounting his horse rode in icy silence back to Windsor Castle where he shut himself in his chamber for the rest of the day and refused to admit anyone to his presence.

A month later he repudiated the Charter. It was wrung from him, he said, by force and in a final defiant gesture he took the Cross, pledging himself to go on crusade so that no Christian man might lift a hand against him.

William Marshal the younger confronted his father at their London home. 'This is past enduring! Is he mad to deny all that he has promised? My lord, you must see we cannot keep from war.'

War?' his father echoed. 'Against the King? You know that I will never raise my sword against him.'

'But our charter? I think he never intended to keep his word and now he is foresworn and God will punish him.'

'Then leave it to God in His own time. The archbishop and I will do our best to persuade the King to reconsider but you know him. It will take time and patience.'

'And we have neither,' his son flashed back. 'You must be less acute than you used to be, my lord, if you think to persuade that madman. He will not listen to you, nor to any man, and if he will not renew his promises made at Running Meade –' He broke off. 'Father, you must join me now. Your word would carry more weight than any.'

William looked at his angry son, affection warring with stubborn loyalty. 'Dear lad, do you think this difference between us does not wound me – your mother also? I would be at one with you if I could – indeed I agree with every word of your charter. But I am a Plantagenet man and have been since I was a mere boy. I have the King's son in my care – one more of old King Henry's house – and I would be less than nothing to myself if I betrayed, now, all that I have given a lifetime's service for.'

The younger William's eyes filled, but the tears were immediately repressed. 'Jesu,' he said in a low voice, 'what has this wretched King brought us to? But we who oppose him are determined. If he will not meet our terms we must resort to other measures.'

'What measures?' his father asked uneasily.

'There is King Philip's son, the Dauphin Louis – a better man than his father, and his wife is a Plantagenet, old King Henry's grand-daughter. Maybe he would make a better King than –'

'Never!' William felt the hot blood rise in his own cheeks and his hand went instinctively to his sword hilt. 'Never! If you are considering that, we shall maybe cross swords, my son.'

'I know. I know and I am sorry for it. But it was you who taught me I must live by my conscience.' They stared at each other for a moment of silence, and in that silence were aware of Isabel standing on the stairs. She had heard their voices in argument and come down only half dressed, a cloak thrown hastily over her white kirtle. Her face was very pale as she looked at her son.

'Your father will not change his mind once it is made up,' she said.

But the younger William was equally stubborn. Without another word he came forward, embraced his father and left the house.

William sank down in his chair, his eyes fixed on the window that gave out on to a small courtyard. He saw his son mount and ride away under the arch. He sat there for a long time, this last grief hard to bear. Presently Isabel came – no word of reproach for him this time – and she knelt beside his chair, her head on his shoulder while he put his arm about her.

On a day that reminded William of that livid storm on the Irish Sea he followed a sick and beaten King on a wild ride northwards. It was not the first time he had enacted this scene, but whereas all his sympathy had lain with the Old King he had none for this, the last and most perverse of his sons.

A long train of knights, men-at-arms and creaking wagons stretched out along the road from Weisbeck, making for the Wash and the crossing over the sands where the Wellstream flowed into the sea.

'We can cross it at low tide,' Randulph de Blundevill said. 'Your grace will be in Sleaford by nightfall.'

John grunted. He had gout in one foot and it was swathed in bandages, supported free from the stirrup, and the skin of his face had an unhealthy yellowish tinge. Every now and again he turned to be sure that the slow, unwieldy wagons were following.

'We would make better time if we left the baggage train to come on at its own pace,' William had suggested this morning. John had given him a cursory glance, muttering that he ought to know better than to suggest that, and even when William offered to put his own nephew in charge of it, the King refused.

Now William tried once more. 'Sire, we should hurry on at a better pace than this. The King of Scots is only too ready to join with your enemies and we must lie between them.'

'Do not tell me what I already know,' John snapped. There was a burning pain in his large stomach and he felt sick but there was a restlessness, a determination in him now that reminded William of the Old King. 'I'll not have the wagons separated from us. If I lose them I lose all. God curse those stupid dolts, can't they make the horses move faster? Or have they harnessed spavined wrecks to my treasure?'

'The horses are good enough,' the Earl of Chester said gloomily. 'It is the loads, my lord. They are too heavy. My lord Pembroke is right, we should have left some of those chests with the monks at Waltham.'

John ground his teeth. 'For the French to plunder? God's wounds, no!' His face convulsed with rage and his voice rose. Will none of you support me, none of you see what must be done? Jesu, what friends I have!'

No one answered him and the slow procession moved on at a pace that tried William's patience almost to breaking point. With all his long experience he was sharply aware of their danger. For months now there had been war in England. The rebel barons, unable to wring any concessions from John, unable to believe anything he said, had – as the younger William said they would – called for help from France. At this moment the Dauphin Louis and his troops were in Kent, marching northwards having by-passed Dover Castle where Hubert de Burgh held out for the King. John became like a cornered bull. He struck out at any of the rebel levies wherever he might find them, laying waste the countryside indiscriminately, burning crops, slaying innocent peasants, blind to the fact that it was his own land he was despoiling. He would not listen to William yet he clung to him, to his loyalty, knowing that there were few such men left to him. His trusted half-brother Salisbury had been captured in France and as negotiations for his release were still going on he was sadly missed by the King's company.

William wondered if together he and Salisbury might have turned John from his suicidal course, the last and most crazy order being to bring most of his treasure, crown and sceptre, gold and jewels, swords and goblets and plate, chests of coins, all packed into the wagons which every day the King checked and counted. If it had been left in safe hands, in the royal vaults at Winchester or with the trustworthy monks of Waltham, they might have made the necessary speed, but John would not listen.

Throughout this wretched time William had felt miserably

alone, none of his old friends with him, nor his sons, for William was still with the rebels and Richard he had sent to France to safeguard his inheritance at Longueville. Only his nephews and John d'Erleigh remained of those he most cared for. And in all this bloody campaign he had done only one thing against John's interests. When the Earl of Chester went to besiege a party of rebels at Worcester, knowing that his son was there and well aware of de Blundevill's methods, he had contrived to send a message to William to warn him. He was thankful the boy had escaped the city and thankful too that Isabel and the younger children were at Exeter with the Queen, far from the area of any fighting.

There was a grey lowering sky today, heavy clouds sweeping up, and he surmised there would be rain before nightfall. They had reached the shallows where it was possible to cross, and the wide sands looked peaceful enough. The wind was blowing fresh and salty from the sea, the flat marshy countryside boasting only a few stunted trees, bent in the direction of the prevailing wind. The guards ahead entered the waters first, the horses' hooves squelching in the soft sand and mud, and the King and his companions followed. William wrapped his cloak about him against the stiffening October wind, cold from the North Sea, and soon they were moving up the higher ground on the further shore.

It was not a place William knew and as they turned back to watch the wagons entering the water he glanced towards the opening of the estuary to the sea and there saw the tide moving in to meet the outflowing of the river.

'Look,' he said and pointed. 'The tide has turned, sire.'

'They'll be across in time,' John muttered. He swung his horse's head round and jerking his gouty leg, cursed. For Christ's sake, move. Are they all stupid, mindless churls?

Move, damn you!'

The men in the water were doing their best, whipping the horses, but the poor beasts, struggling with loads beyond their strength, heaved in vain as the wheels sank into the treacherous sands. Only two wagons had reached the safety of firm ground.

'Go back,' de Blundevill shouted and calling to a soldier ordered him to go down and command the rest to retreat to the shore behind.

'No! No!' the King countermanded. 'I'll not have it. They must cross before the tide comes – there's time yet.'

'Holy God!' It was the King's cousin, Earl William of Warenne, who pointed to the east, the colour ebbing from his face. 'Look, my lord – look there. What in God's name is happening?'

The tide was suddenly running with a force no one had suspected, though the sullen peasants who had been robbed to feed them as they passed could have told them. It came sweeping in to meet the river in a headlong clash, the water deepening every moment, the swirling and threshing made worse today by the rising wind, the approaching storm.

In minutes the shallows were lost. The horses struggled desperately in their harness, some of the drivers clung still to the reins, but others leapt in terror into the current and were swept away. Wagons toppled, boxes burst open, gold plates and jewels, chests of silver, all the insignia of royalty burst out, floating ludicrously for a moment before being immersed in tossing foam. Horses sank, the wagons after them, as the angry sea beat in against the river; the tide, the wind, and the first driving rain winning a hideous victory.

In what seemed an incredible and horrific onslaught of nature, lasting so short a time, almost all of the baggage train was gone leaving a pathetic flotsam, a few bodies that tossed wildly until they too disappeared, until nothing remained of all the King's treasure.

John sat his horse, ashen and mesmerised, shivering with cold, his eyes fixed on one stray goblet bobbing on the waves until at last that too disappeared from sight. His attendants watched him, equally horror-struck, until at last he turned away and rode north through the mist and rain.

The Earls of Chester and Pembroke had always disliked each other heartily, but now they were forced into an odd comradeship as it soon became clear that John was not only suffering from shock at this final blow but was gravely ill as well. At Sleaford he had a high fever, but when William suggested the next morning that he should remain in bed in the castle there, he groaned and swore, vomited and then called for a horse litter to take him on to Newark.

'He is dying,' de Blundevill said and William nodded. He had seen that look on men's faces often enough to recognise it now in the King's bloated features.

At Newark John was carried into the Bishop's Palace, the storm still raging, wind and rain beating at the shutters. He asked the Bishop to hear his confession and the two Earls withdrew to an outer chamber.

William sat down wearily by the fire. He seldom wore full armour now except for battle, preferring a padded gambeson and a tunic. He suffered from stiffness in the back and this last ride through the driving rain had set his bones aching.

De Blundevill found some wine and poured it. 'If he is to confess all his sins we are like to be here for some time,' he said and laughed coarsely. 'Long enough for us to have dinner, eh?'

He stumped off, shouting for the steward, but William

went instead to the chapel where he knelt for a long time, thinking less of the dying King than of England, of Pembroke that he had come to love so much, of Caversham and his other lands, of Isabel and the children who would inherit all he had won. The King's heir was a nine-year-old boy and might bring worse feuding upon this poor land, and William braced himself, praying that despite his years he might still do something to bring back order and peace; he had known little of it in his own lifetime.

Presently a frightened clerk came to say the King wanted him. He went back and found John lying quieter, though his breathing was laboured, and there was a nauseating smell of sickness and decay in the room.

'William.' He stretched out a hot, sweating hand. 'You have never failed my house and now I leave my son in your hands. Care for him – go to him at once – promise me.'

'I swear it,' William said. It seemed to him that all the rites of Holy Church, the holy water sprinkled here, could not wash away the sense of evil about this man. Yet a crucifix lay on his breast and his other hand plucked at it.

'Your son shall be King,' William said steadily. 'You can be at peace for him, sire.'

John's eyes closed. William glanced at the Bishop, who shook his head. Suddenly the King's lids rose for the last time. 'Why did nobody tell me about the tide? If we had known – all my treasure – all lost. God was angry – or was it the devil?' His face convulsed once more and then his head fell to one side.

The Bishop laid an expert hand on the King's breast, touched his mouth and began the prayers for the dead.

'Well, thank God for that,' de Blundevill muttered under his breath and then hastily crossed himself.

In the great cathedral of Gloucester the young King Henry III was crowned by the Bishop of Winchester in the presence of the few nobles who were quickly gathered there before the throne could be offered to Louis of France.

The royal crown was at the bottom of the Wash so a plain gold circlet was set on Henry's bright head and when it was done, William Marshal held him high to face the assembled barons.

'My lords,' he cried out, 'this boy is truly King of England, crowned and anointed. Do not visit on him the sins of his father. By God's grace he will be a good King to us.'

There was an answering shout and the young King, set on his feet again, held out his hands as the Earl Marshal knelt before him, the first to do him homage. 'My lord,' he said in his clear boy's voice, 'I thank God that I have you to advise me – by His mercy we will do well together.'

William kissed the small hand. He was seventy-two and this child was nine and it seemed to him it would be better if other, younger men took on the task.

But a few days later, at a great meeting where all but the most recalcitrant lords deserted their French allies and came to pay homage to the new King, with one voice they all united in insisting that no man was fitter than the Earl of Pembroke to be Regent of England during the King's minority. Even the surly Earl of Chester added his voice, swearing he would serve under the Marshal, and a final exhortation came from the Papal Legate.

'My lords,' William protested, 'I am too old. I have seen too much and I am tired.'

One by one they pressed about him, friends and late enemies alike, his own sons and sons-in-law among the most vociferous, refusing to listen to his reasons nor to pay account to his years. For a moment he ceased to hear their voices, his mind going back over many of those years.

Four kings he had served and now a fifth commanded his loyalty, and he remembered that other King, Stephen, who had prevented a group of ruthless men from hanging him. Stephen had preserved him for a long life culminating in this final achievement, and he put up his hand once more to touch the amethyst brooch, feeling the gems fashioning the sprig of *planta genesta*. He remembered Queen Eleanor at her loveliest and he an untried lad without a penny in his pocket. Never had he dreamed then that he would become Regent of England, virtual ruler of his country, and the trust of these tough fighting barons stirred him. He wondered what the Old King would have thought of it, that man of tremendous vitality. He thought too of his young master, so full of promise, whom he had loved and who had died so tragically in his arms, of Richard whom he had never loved but deeply respected, John whom he had served despite his personal dislike.

Now it was all to begin again and for a moment he shrank from it. He had thought now that the new King was crowned perhaps he could retire to Pembroke or Caversham and spend his days quietly, enjoying things he had never had time for before, but this dream was to have no reality. He must bring order and peace back to the country, and surely if the task was to be laid on him God would give him the strength for it?

He looked down at the little King, seated in a great chair, scarlet legs not reaching the floor, and in a sudden lift of the head saw a remarkable likeness to his master of long ago. He had never cared for any man as he had cared for the Young King and now it was as if he was to serve him once more in this boy who was so like him.

Glancing up at the gallery where his wife and daughters sat with the widowed Queen he saw Matilda's face alight with pleasure, but there was anxiety as well as pride on his wife's well-loved features and he gave her a reassuring smile.

'Well, my lords,' he said at last, 'it seems it is not yet time for me to take my old bones to the fireside. If it is your will that I accept this high office, so be it. What years I have left,' he smiled down at the eager boy, 'are yours to command sire.'

AUTHOR'S NOTE

William Marshal died two years later at Caversham, adopting the habit of the Knights Templar a few days before his death. He had kept his word and reunited the kingdom, seeing the boy King set firmly on the throne, terms made with the French that shamed no one. He was buried at his own request in the Temple Church in London, and hearing of his passing King Philip said, 'He was the most loyal knight I have ever known.' It is an odd fact that none of William's sons had children, thus fulfilling the curse of the Bishop of Ferns. The office of Marshal passed through his daughter to her son Roger Bigod, Earl of Norfolk, in which family it has stayed to the present day.

THE PLANTAGENET LINE
CONTINUES

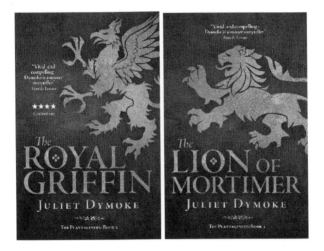

On sale from Amazon